A Gangsta's Bitch

Leo Sullivan

A Gangsta's Bitch

Sullivan Productions, Films and Literacy, LLC

PO Box 1342

Decatur, GA 30031-1342

www.Leolsullivan.com

Cover Design/Graphics: Marion Designs

Author: Leo Sullivan

Printed in the United States of America

IN LOVING MEMORY OF MY MOTHER
EVETTE L. SULLIVAN
AUGUST 7, 1947 – JUNE 9, 2006

May your beautiful soul rest in peace and the legacy of your loving grace live on.

Dear Mama,
I never had a chance to say goodbye,
to tell you just how much I love you.
My mind still refuses to accept the fact that you are gone.
This is the most difficult writing I've ever had to incite
Through misty eyes, my pen flows ink in tears.
God only knows how many times I've attempted to write this…
It's hard Mama.
Some say my mother died from malpractice,
a hospital's negligence.
Some say she died from an internal illness…
I am sure my mother died like millions of other Black women,
from a lack of love, loneliness and a broken heart.
I, her only child, should have been there for her.

THREE CAN KEEP A SECRET IF TWO ARE DEAD

A GANGSTA'S BITCH

Jack and Gina

They were illegally parked in front of the Galaxy Hotel in Brooklyn. A million and one thoughts presented themselves in Jack's mind – thoughts born from the sheer determination to survive in a vortex of hell, in a place called Brooklyn. Like most young gods, Jack had received most of his education in a 10' x 12'cell, haunted by white angry faces and blatant racists, in a place where men learned to be men. The system had brilliantly orchestrated a plan, a mental murder for hire. They tried to kill his spirit, break his soul, but in the end, they were forced to admit: young black men were resilient like an army of project roaches. They say one of the worst things you can do is lock a man up all day and have him do nothing but think. Think about how he got caught. Think about how to get away next time. Think about revenge. Think about the crazy statistic that said 74% of black men who got out of prison came back within eighteen months of their release. Damn!

While they plotted his mental demise, Jack created a disguise by reading many books that taught him how to outwit the man. He read books on revolutionaries like George Jackson, Malcolm X and Nat Turner. Jack read so many books, that the words would come to life and talk to him. They sharpened his mind, showing him how to avoid ever coming back to prison. Soon

Jack learned that a man who doesn't plan, plans to fail. For some reason, everyone started calling him a Thug Revolutionist. That was around the time Jack won his appeal and was released from federal prison where he had been serving a life sentence. It was on!

One

It was five o'clock in the morning and Gina had just built up enough courage to tell Jack that she was tired. Her feet hurt from walking all night in stilettos. She wanted nothing else but to go home, take a long, hot shower and get into her comfortable bed.

She looked into his handsome face, but his eyes were trained on the entrance of the hotel. Etched on his face was an expression of deep concentration, unblinking, unfailing.

"There! There!" He spotted his target. "There the nigga go right there," Jack said, exercising extreme calm, the kind an experienced hunter uses when stalking prey.

Gina's body perked up and she became alert and focused as she slid her eyes off Jack, and over to Damon Dice, one of the richest niggas in New York City. Instantly, she felt a rush of high-octane adrenaline. She was about to become the kind of weapon a man uses when he'd rather have court on the streets. Court would soon be in session, with Jack being both judge and jury.

"Listen Gina," Jack spoke, never taking his eyes off Damon.

"You gotta get this nigga to walk you close to the car so I can get his testifying ass in the trunk." His tone was hushed and his forehead knotted.

For the past three days, they had been tailing Damon Dice and his entourage. Earlier that night, they had been in a club called The Tunnel in Manhattan. It was the spot where all the ballers, shot callers and entertainers were known to mingle. That night the place was jam-packed. The music was pumping bass so hard that Gina could feel its pulsating rhythm in her chest. Somehow, it seemed to hype her up as all the colorful lights strobed throughout the club. She strained her eyes in search of her target.

Finally, she spotted him and the big-ass platinum chain around his neck. Scantily dressed in a chic tight miniskirt that showed off all of her goodies and accentuated her plump round ass, she slowly sashayed toward him, sensuously moving her hips from side to side. She wasn't wearing a bra and her see-through silk blouse left little to the imagination as her gorgeous breasts rose upward in salute to her youth. Boldly, Gina strutted into the VIP section of the club as if she belonged there, walking right up to Damon Dice and his crew. All eyes were on her. Show time! All their mouths dropped like old folks with lockjaw.

Get the nigga to follow you out da club, Gina heard Jack's words in her mind as she neared Damon, never taking her eyes off him. She arched her back, thrusting her mouth-watering nipples forward, parallel to Damon's eyes. He sat in his seat staring at her, mouth agape, drink in hand. As she approached she held him spellbound. All the members of his crew were also entranced. Her sweet perfume marinated their nostrils as she bent down showing them some peek-a-boo cleavage.

Coyly, she whispered in Damon's ear, her lips brushing against his earlobe, "Nigga, I'll suck that dick so good your balls will get jealous." Damon choked on his drink, accidentally spitting on his boy sitting next to him, who erupted in laughter.

Damn, this chick is bold, he thought as he watched Gina.

"I got the world's best pussy."

He could have sworn he saw one of her nipples wink at him as he took in all of her audacious, shapely curves. That was around the time he got an erection.

They struck up a conversation and the drinks began to flow. She cozied up to him, flirting and touching, doing all the things that Jack had told her to do. She played her part well. Stealthily, Gina would reach her hand under the table and play with his dick, stroking him as she poured a heavy dose of her feminine charm all over him. Finally, she had cast her spell. She could see it in his eyes. He was filled with lust and enchanted by her beauty. If she wanted to, she could have fucked him right there on the dance floor.

Ever so gently, she took his hand, the fox leading the chicken, and moved past his bodyguards and crew of henchmen. She led him toward the dance floor with him palming her ass like two basketballs. Drunk, he followed as if he were a lost child. As they passed through the crowd, they headed for the exit. Slyly, Gina smiled as she thought about Jack waiting outside.

All of a sudden, five yards from the door, all hell broke loose. A salvo of gunshots rang out causing pandemonium. Like a scared rabbit, Damon Dice didn't even try to protect her. He just took off running back to the safety of his bodyguards.

"Punk-ass nigga," Gina cursed as she ducked down and headed for the exit door.

Two

Damion Dice

Damon staggered out of the Galaxy Hotel, intoxicated by a cocktail of exotic drugs. He wore so much heavy jewelry that when he walked he made loud metallic clinging sounds. Animated, he wobbled over to the wall and grabbed hold of it as if he were trying to stop the building from falling. The front of his pants were soiled with a large piss stain that ran the length of his left pant leg. That night he was faced with one of the biggest dilemmas of the day – should he take his dick out and piss right there in front of the hotel or vomit first?

With his world spinning, his bodily functions didn't give him a chance to decide. With his dick in his hand, he began to vomit and urinate uncontrollably. It truly was a sight to behold.

Afterwards, with his mouth ringed with vomit, he staggered away while trying to place his joint back into his pants. He looked up, and through bleary eyes, he saw Gina floating toward him. He tried his best to stand up straight, but the damn building kept leaning to the side.

Damn, she fine as a muthafucka, he thought as she sauntered up close. He tried to wipe his mouth with his shirt sleeve and smile. Even in the dim light, he could still make out the symmetry of her body. He staggered slightly in a failed attempt to gain his equilibrium.

"Heyyy fella!" Gina caroled seductively in a breathy voice as she walked up to him, enrapturing him with the wiles of her charm.

"Damn … you the broad … I mean … ahh … uhh," Damon stammered as he recalled seeing her.

His mouth was still partially ringed with vomit. Everything was still spinning, but starting to slow down. He let go of the wall, his legs wobbling unsteadily like a child just learning to walk. Gina came closer. He reached out and fondled one of her lovely breasts. She rewarded him with a giggle as jubilant as a young schoolgirl on her first date. She furtively glanced over her shoulder at Jack hunched low in the car watching her every move.

"Shorty, you wanna come inside the telly? A nigga got everything you need. You like to smoke? I got … I got …" Drunk, Damon lost his train of thought as he scratched his head. "I got what you need," Damon said, causing Gina to tentatively take a step back.

Goddamn! His breath smell just like horse shit, she thought as she noticed a puddle of vomit on the ground in front of him. It took everything in her power not to frown as he once again caressed her breasts. Talk about being an actress—she deserved an Oscar.

"I would love to come inside," she drawled. "You still want me to suck that dick?"

She licked her lips and reached down to rub him. As she did that, she felt a wet spot. Nasty muthafucka, she thought to herself as she removed her hand and placed it on her shirt, slyly wiping her hand.

"Big daddy, why don't you walk me to my car first, to lock it up … tight," she cajoled, puckering her luscious lips, showing him one of her sex faces.

"Wha … wha … where ya parked at, shorty?" Damon asked.

She giggled innocently, taking his hand and walking him toward Jack in the parked car. He staggered a few steps and suddenly stopped in his tracks. His eyes popped open as if he'd seen a ghost. He stared at something in the distance. Whatever it was spooked him, causing him to sober up quickly.

"Naw shorty. I just saw something across the street. A light went on in that van."

He squinted his eyes as if trying to focus in his inebriated fog. Damon pulled away from her hand and started to backpedal out of her grasp.

Not again, Gina thought as she remembered the scene back at the club and how mad Jack was with her for letting him get away.

Think fast! Think fast! Trick-ass nigga getting away! Her mind churned. She reached into her purse and pulled out an elegant gold-plated .357 Derringer pistol. It was the size of a Bic lighter, but powerful enough to drop an elephant.

"Take another step, bitch-ass nigga, and I'ma blow your whole fuckin' back out. Now try me!" she said coldly between clinched teeth. Her face was a mask of deadly intent.

For some reason, in her mind, everything moved in slow, surreal motion. A lavender sky was starting to peek over the pitch black horizon as dawn, like a dirty sheet on the canvas of the night, exposed the good, the bad and the ugly. In the distance, birds were starting to chirp, summoning morning.

"Pah-pah-leese don't shoot me!" Damon begged.

They were standing only inches apart. A lone car passed, and its luminous headlights traced their bodies stalled in the night. The air suddenly turned cool with the imminent threat of death. Sweat gleamed on Damon's forehead as he stood panic-stricken, overcome with fear. Gina could tell he was thinking about bolting. There was no doubt whatsoever in her mind—if Damon tried to get away, she would kill him.

The lobby doors opened and out walked Damon's bodyguard. The man was huge. He stood about six feet, seven inches, three hundred and something pounds. He had broad shoulders like a mountain. The man's name was Prophet. He was an ex-con and a well-known killer. As soon as Prophet got out the joint, Damon Dice gave him a job as head of DieHard Security. Next to Prophet stood G-Solo, who was slightly built, with a baby face and long eyelashes. He resembled the rapper Chingy. Both men were strapped with guns.

"Yo, son! What the fuck is going on out here?" Prophet asked suspiciously as he took a step closer.

His deep, throaty baritone voice seemed to resonate with the timbre of a man that commanded authority.

Playfully, Gina laughed and hugged Damon as she placed the barrel of the gun against his rib cage and whispered in his ear as Prophet approached, "Tell them you'll be inside in a second."

"I'ma … I'ma … I'ma be inside in a second," the frightened man said, raising his voice.

"Nigga, you know you got on too much ice," Prophet warned as he stepped closer. He was only a few feet from Gina now. "Come on man, let's go."

"You fitna be shittin' in a plastic bag, rollin' around in a wheelchair," Gina whispered in Damon's ear, feeling Prophet's presence was too damn close. She pushed the gun harder against his ribs.

"Man! I told 'cha, I'm fuckin' coming! Leave me the fuck alone!" Damon yelled at his bodyguard, causing him to exchange looks with G-Solo.

They both shrugged their shoulders as if to say, 'fuck him, let him have his way with the bitch' as they walked away.

Gina could feel Damon's arms shaking like leaves on a tree.

"Pah-pah-pahleese don't kill me," Damon pleaded.

"Shut up, nigga!" Gina said as she peeked over in Jack's direction, huddled in the car.

Just then, a weary crackhead prostitute walked up. She was dressed in raggedy clothes – a pair of blue jeans that looked like they had not been washed in days, sneakers and a once-white halter top that was now gray. Her eyes continued to dart suspiciously back and forth across the street as she smacked her lips as if she had just bitten into a sour lemon.

She jerked her long neck, snaking it from side to side hyperactively with her hand poised on her body as she patted her foot on the concrete. On a crackhead's impulse, her eyes began to search the ground as if this was the sacred ground where she had lost her rock the other night.

Her foot did a casual sweep of the pavement as she made a face, twisting her lips as she said matter-of-factly, "Girlfriend, I think that's the po-po across the street parked in that van."

Hearing that caused Damon's body to flinch uncontrollably.

"Shit!" Gina muttered as she glanced over at the white van.

Why didn't I recognize it earlier? she thought.

"I'ma scream if you don't let me go," Damon whimpered.

Something about hearing the word "police" had emboldened him.

"Nigga, you stunt if you wanna, and I'ma leave your punk ass slumped right here with a hole in your chest!" Gina hissed as she cocked the gun and pressed it harder against his ribs.

Damon was standing on the balls of his feet as if that would ease the explosion if the gun went off, shattering his rib cage and blowing his whole back out.

The prostitute continued to look back and forth in all directions, including the ground, akin to a junkie's perpetual paranoia.

Once again Gina glanced over at the car with Jack in it and then looked at the undercover police van.

"Shit!"

Three

"Unit six to Captain Brooks …"

"Go ahead, this is Captain Brooks," an authoritative voice returned over the sporadic crackling of the police radio.

"Lieutenant Stanley Goldstein is trying to reach you on your cell phone."

Brooks turned on his cell and it rang instantly. The Lieutenant spoke urgently. "The suspect and his entourage have just turned off Pennsylvania Avenue onto Linden and Stanley. They're at the Galaxy Hotel."

"You're in fuckin' Brooklyn now?" Captain Brooks shrieked over the phone, thinking about the friction it would cause with the 75th Precinct. They already had a bad rivalr y, and this would only make things worse.

"I want you and the rest of the unit to stay clear of the suspect until I get there and give the order to take his black ass down," the Captain barked over the phone.

"Captain?"

"What?" Brooks answered brusquely.

"Sir, there appears to be a white Cadillac with a black female driving. There is also another individual in the car that we can't seem to make out. They have been trailing the suspect all night long. The car is now illegally parked in front of the hotel. How shall we proceed?"

"Leave the car alone. We don't want to risk tipping off the 75th that we're on their turf about to make a major bust. They're probably harmless groupies. Tell your men to hang tight. I'm on my way." Brooks hung up the phone and made a U-turn in the middle of the street.

As he drove, his mind went over every detail as it related to how he was going to make the bust. Damon Dice was actually out of Brooks' jurisdiction, but since his department had tailed him from Manhattan to Brooklyn in violation of possession of drugs, the arrest was going to be perfectly legal. Now all Brooks had to do was plant the dope.

The good thing about what he was doing was that the Mayor himself was behind the special task force to arrest as many rappers as they could, and so far so good. His depar tment had been having a field day. The only thing that kept Damon Dice on the streets for so long was the fact that he was a police informant and had been giving Brooks information for a long time. That was until he turned music mogul.

Damon Dice had switched hats from hustler to entrepreneur in the blink of an eye. He now felt he was invincible and refused to provide Brooks with any helpful information. Brooks hated that he didn't bust Damon earlier. Now he was selling hit records just like Suge Knight and J. Prince.

This fueled Brooks even more as his nondescript Ford sliced through the night. What really pissed him off was to see a black man making so much damn money, legally. They were becoming a threat. Hell, the rapper 40, one of the hottest in the industry, had just bought a mansion with forty rooms, a bowling alley and a movie theater. Another was partial owner of a basketball team. It was becoming a trend.

How do they do it? he pondered.

His knuckles were white as he tightly held onto the steering wheel as the car reached speeds of over a hundred miles per hour. He was consumed with the anticipation of the bust. He felt the adrenaline of a policeman's head rush – the set-up, the chase, the capture and then the arrest. Just the thought of it gave him an erection. He would teach the fucker who he was playing with.

Besides, Brooks wanted to please the Mayor. He was already told to treat all rappers as potential drug dealers until proven differently. Now, all he had to do was follow the first law of police work—if there isn't a crime, invent one.

Captain Brooks made the excursion from Manhattan to Brooklyn in seventeen minutes flat. Lights out, he cruised past the White Castle restaurant where a few prostitutes loitered.

Unbeknownst to him, somewhere, somehow in the hub of this naked city, the streets were watching, waiting, listening. Brooks eased his car behind another unmarked car. As he exited, a dog barked in the distance. A crescent moon, embellished with stars, hung from the night sky like a lucid scratch on the underbelly of the black canvas of the night.

A weary prostitute ambled by. The woman took one look at the supposed undercover cop and decided he damn sure was not a trick. She took off walking fast, looking over her shoulder as if to make sure the cop made no attempt to tackle her.

The night air felt crisp and cool against Brooks' pale skin as he walked toward the surveillance van. He realized that he was starting to sweat under his cotton shirt, causing it to stick to his skin.

The foul odor of rotten garbage mixed with New York air pollution, only seemed to enhance the moment. Eyes alert, he could feel his senses tingling as he felt for the ounce of crack he had in his pocket. He intended to plant the dope on Damon Dice. That would get his ass to talking.

Lieutenant Goldstein opened the van door. Brooks grunted as he squatted, struggling to get in. The forty or so pounds he had picked up over the last few years were starting to take their toll on him. There were four other undercover officers in the cramped van.

"Captain, I just received word from the 75th Precinct. They want to know what we're doing on their turf. They're asking us to back off and let them handle the arrest."

"Handle my ass! I'm in command here. My authority comes all the way from the Mayor's office," Brooks screeched. He thought about the dope in his pocket intended for Damon Dice.

"Tell whomever it is that I said to fuck him and the horse he rode in on!"

"Holy shit!" one of the undercover officers lamented as he looked through the night vision binoculars.

Brooks snatched the binoculars and peered out the window. As he bent down he accidentally hit a light switch causing the inside of the van to light up.

And as usual, the streets were watching.

Four

Jack and Gina

Gina stood in front of the Galaxy Hotel paralyzed with fear as she held the gun against Damon's ribs. The prostitute had just warned her that the police were parked across the street in the van.

Jack had spied everything from the confines of the car, but he had no idea that the police were parked nearby watching them.

Don't panic, Gina thought as her mind frantically searched for a way out, but it was useless, at least for her. Now her main concern was for Jack. They both didn't have to go to prison, if she could help it. She fully intended to save him by any means necessary. Suddenly, she had an idea.

"Give her all your money," Gina ordered, shoving the gun harder against his ribs.

"What?" Damon asked.

"Nigga, you heard me!" Gina raised her voice.

The prostitute continued to look on. Three people walked out of the hotel, a woman and two men. The woman saw what was going on, but played it off as she quickened her pace and nudged one of her partners. They saw, but didn't see. In the real world of the ghetto, a hero gets punished, sometimes even killed, for interfering in other people's business.

The threesome passed on their way to the parking garage.

Damon's hands were shaking so bad when he handed the prostitute the wad of cash that the diamond platinum bracelets on his arms chimed like bells. He gave the junkie a little over six thousand dollars.

"Listen, you got a family?" Gina asked the prostitute.

"Yeah, I got a three-year-old girl," the junkie replied, eyes as big as silver dollars as she licked her dry lips.

"I have a family, too," Gina said as she spied the van across the street. "That's my family parked in that white car across the street over there." Gina pointed with a nod of her head. "I want you to promise me that you'll take that money and do something for your kid. But first I want you to walk over there and tell that dude parked in the car…tell him to go. Tell him the police are watching us, like a set up. Tell him the spot is hot. Tell him…" Gina's voice cracked. "Tell him I love him."

Why Gina just didn't walk away and let Damon go was a mystery. It was as if she couldn't stop, not even if she wanted to. Since Jack had gone away, robbery was in her blood and rushed through her veins. Every fiber in her body needed the feel of command over another's soul. Damon was the fix for her addiction.

Hauntingly, she was often reminded of a story she had watched as a small child on television, on PBS. It was a horrific story about how African monkeys are hunted, trapped and killed. The hunter merely places a shiny object inside a cage and the monkey reaches inside the cage to grab the shiny object. It's too big to get out of the narrow bars of the cage, and when the hunters come to trap him, even at the risk of his own life, the monkey is too dumb to let go, and is ultimately killed for refusing to let go.

Like the monkey, Gina refused to let go, and she knew some day it would cost her, her life.

She spun Damon around and made mock laughter like the two of them were lovebirds having a friendly frolic. She walked him toward the parking garage. There, she intended to strip him like a stolen Chevy.

Inside the dark garage, the stench of piss was strong. As she continued to walk him like a dog in the dim light, her mind raced.

How was she going to pull this off? The entire time, Damon whimpered and pleaded for his life.

Suddenly up ahead, car lights flashed and tires screeched.

Startled, she braced herself as she held Damon by his shirt, leveling the gun at his kidneys. The car continued to accelerate toward her, its headlights engulfing them like deer standing in the middle of the road.

Police!

Gina feared.

The car came to a screeching halt, only inches in front of them. Jack jumped out wearing a ski mask and a bullet-proof vest.

He rushed over to her and pointed the AK-47 at Damon's head.

For the second time that day, Damon pissed in his pants.

A few yards away a woman screamed. It was the same woman that had passed Gina earlier with her two companions. They were about to enter a cream-colored Lexus. The woman continued to scream. Jack rushed over to her and smacked her upside the head with the butt of his gun. Silence. She dropped like a sack of rocks as her two companions grimaced in horror.

"Gimme your car keys and wallets!" Jack commanded. His voice echoed.

Terror-stricken, both men complied. Jack was moving fast as Gina looked on. "Remember, I got your IDs, so I know how to find you. Lie on the ground and be quiet for five minutes."

Both men obeyed and lay down on the pissy concrete. Jack quickly moved to the back of the Lexus, opening the trunk with the car keys. He pointed the gun at Damon, waving for Gina to come on.

Damon was moving too slow, so she shoved him so hard he nearly fell as he stumbled. Gina marched him over to the open trunk.

"Girl, what the fuck you tryna do? You fuckin' death struck or somethin'?" Jack said as he hit Damon in the head with the butt of his gun. As Damon fell, Gina tried to grab him by his shirt, but it tore and Damon hit his head on the concrete with a thud.

Moving swiftly, together they hoisted his body into the trunk as they both heard the blare of police sirens. Alarmed, they looked at each other. Jack threw her the car keys. "It's on you, Ma. If they open up the trunk I'm comin' out blastin'." He dived into the trunk next to the unconscious Damon Dice.

Gina slammed the trunk shut, ran and jumped into the front seat. Placing the key in the ignition, she took a deep breath in an attempt to calm her nerves. She pulled off and headed toward the exit.

In front of her, lights bleared as sirens shrilled in her ears. Up ahead a caravan of police cars raced toward her.

It ain't gonna fuckin' go down like this, she thought as her heart pounded so hard in her chest that it felt like it was going to explode.

A police car pulled in front of her, blocking her path. Gina clinched the gun in her hand as she thought about Jack in the trunk. Two police officers hopped out of their patrol cars with guns drawn, aimed at her head. "Get out of the car! Get out of the car, now!" One officer was white, the other black.

Gina palmed the small gun in her hand. Her life flashed before her eyes, the monkey that couldn't let go. Her mind churned, Think fast! Think fast!

"Nooo! Nooo!" she cried hysterically.

"There's a masked gunman back there! He tried to kidnap me! He already has one hostage back there with him."

She pointed with her hand as the other clasped the gun between her legs as she continued to cry the way only a black woman could to save her man and herself. She manufactured an ocean of tears, with a 'please help me, woman in distress' face to match.

Somehow, Gina was able to melt the heart of the white cop, but the black cop looked at her quizzically.

The white cop looked behind Gina to the other end of the parking garage as he spoke, "I want you to drive out of here to safety and park your car on the side of the building. I'll send an officer to get a description of the gunman."

Gina nodded her head as she listened to the officer give her orders. A dry lump formed in her throat as she swallowed.

"Okay…" she muttered as she listened to the cop call for backup on his radio. He asked for the SWAT team. Gina did as instructed and drove slowly through the throngs of police cars and flashing lights, all the while unconscious of the fact that she was holding her breath and praying to a God that had never listened to her.

Five

Captain Bill Brooks

"What the fuck is going on?" Brooks shrieked, his face flustered as he watched from the concealment of the van.

The pretty black girl and Damon Dice flirted and touched on each other. Then two men walked out. There was an exchange of words. The two men left, a few other people passed and suddenly the crackhead that Brooks had seen earlier was talking to the couple and the pretty black girl walked Damon Dice to the parking garage.

She's probably going to suck his dick, Captain Brooks thought.

Moments later the white car followed the girl into the garage and the next thing Brooks knew all hell broke loose. A woman's scream echoed from the garage and police came from everywhere.

What the hell was the 75th Precinct doing there? The scene was pure madness. The streets were cluttered with police cars from both precincts.

Brooks watched the Lexus slowly drive out of the garage and weave through the congested streets.

"Sir, that's the 75th Precinct," Lieutenant Stanley meekly said to his superior, Captain Brooks.

"Thought I gave you orders to tell them to back the fuck off!"

Brooks spat angrily.

"I did," Stanley barked back, making a face as he scurried to get out of the van.

"Motherfucking bureaucratic bullshit!" Brooks yelled as he got out of the van and stormed over to the handsomely dressed, plainclothes officer who had just arrived on the scene and was giving orders.

"Who's in fucking charge here?" Brooks huffed.

"I am," the handsome black man said as he turned to meet the other man's stare. "And you've just fucked up for not getting permission from 75th."

"Fuck 75th buddy, and you with it. Who the hell are you?"

"Lieutenant Anthony Brown." He pulled out his badge.

"Well, by the time I'm finished with you, you'll be Lieutenant of fucking chicken shit, working somewhere in Alaska!"

Just then, the police radio crackled to life. Lieutenant Brown signaled for one of his men to pass him their radio. "Lieutenant Brown, go ahead."

"There are two males and an unconscious female in here," the voice on the other end replied urgently. "One of the males said an armed gunman hit his girl upside the head and stole their car. The other male claims he doesn't remember what happened. Be advised, a woman and a man were seen placing an individual in the trunk of a stolen beige Lexus. These individuals are to be considered armed and dangerous."

Lieutenant Brown looked over at Captain Brooks as the irate man kicked the side of a car. The voice on the other end of the radio continued, "One of the suspects, the woman, talked her way past a couple of officers. She's driving the Lexus. There is also an abandoned white Cadi—"

"White Cadillac?" Brooks retorted as his eyebrows shot up as he thought about the girl.

She wasn't a groupie, he thought. He now realized she was part of some elaborate robbery scheme. He looked up to see the beige Lexus turning the corner.

"There they go!" he shouted.

As Gina slowly drove away with her human cargo in the trunk, she had no idea just how bad her day was going to get.

Six

The Gentlemen's Club

Monique Cheeks - Fire

Curvaceous hips and sensuous brown thighs gyrated as her soft, honey-colored complexion glistened under the shine of bright lights. Sleek, sable velvet skin radiated beneath perspiration. Monique Cheeks was nude, bare as a baby's ass, as she danced ever so gracefully like a black swan, with the agility of an athlete and limberness of a cat. She bent over backward, lower …lower … each rhythmical beat of the music seemed to challenge her body. She arched her spine. Her titillating body hypnotized the men as she held them, and a few women, spellbound.

With her head nearly touching the floor, she raised her arms flailing like a mermaid in water. Then slowly, as naturally as a kitten yawns, she raised her leg as she held the bottom of her foot with her hand … higher … higher … until finally she had placed her leg on the back of her neck. The room became quiet, lulled to silence as if time stood still.

On one leg, Monique pivoted on the ball of her foot, then her toe. Magnificent! She raised her head to the heavens in a statuesque pose, while her small breasts jetted forward.

The jubilant crowd of wealthy white men erupted with raucous applause that stemmed into a standing ovation. Large streams of money were tossed on stage. The next show had to be delayed as Monique retrieved all the ten, twenty and fifty-dollar bills. There were even a few hundred-dollar bills balled up.

At twenty-one years of age, Monique Cheeks was the first African American woman to ever be given a chance to dance at the prestigious Gentlemen's Club. She did it with an urban hip-hop flare. At first the establishment had no intention of hiring a black woman, but under state laws, for the record, they at least had to make a show of practicing equal employment or risk losing their license. Monique auditioned and danced for the management. They were in awe of her style of dance. The black girl from the Marcus Garvey projects was hired that same day.

For the first time since college she was doing something that she truly loved—dancing. Three years ago, she had won a scholarship to attend the prestigious School of Modern Dance at Yale University. That same year she had become pregnant and was forced to drop out. She and her family were devastated, as the incident stalled what looked like a promising career.

She ended up taking a part-time job at a baker y and hating every minute of it, until one day she saw an ad in the paper: "Dancers wanted. Must be professional."

Desperate to climb out of poverty's perilous grip, in search of a future for her child and herself, she applied for the position. To her surprise, out of twenty women, she was chosen. Now she would have the money to pay for college and move out of the Marcus Garvey projects, where she and her family had lived all their lives, generation to generation.

For the first two months at the Gentlemen's Club, she was treated like an outcast by her co-workers, all except one white girl and she only spoke casually in passing. It didn't really matter to Monique what the rest of the girls thought about her. She knew that she had one clear advantage over them—soul. Monique danced with the soul and rhythm of a black woman and that wasn't something that could be learned. You either had it or you didn't.

However, Monique was forced to notice that some of the most beautiful women in the world worked at the club. Women of all races. Monique started to wonder, "When did white women start having bodies like black women?" Often the white girls danced so off-beat and out-of-sync with the music, it made Monique laugh as a few of the girls actually tried to imitate her.

One thing Monique promised herself was that she would never disgrace herself by opening her legs and dancing nude for a table dance, ridiculing herself like the rest of the girls did for the love of money. She kept it strictly on stage, with the exception of a few select customers, and that was by her own choice. The establishment didn't go along with it at first; however, when they saw that she, alone, could pack a house with urban dance, they were forced to go along with it.

Monique made almost three times the money that the rest of the girls made. On a good night she could easily bring home $3,000. She was also painfully aware that some of the girls had open disdain for that.

One night after she had just finished her show to a standing room only crowd, she gathered her money off the stage floor and went to the ladies' dressing room with the rest of the girls. As usual, some of them spoke and some didn't.

As she passed a few girls to get to her locker, she was horrified to see the words "Nigger Bitch" scrawled on her locker in bold red lipstick. Stunned, Monique stood there as her eyes filled with tears of despair. She wanted nothing more than to be friends with the rest of the girls.

How could someone be so mean? she thought, her heart full of hurt.

Slowly, she turned around in search of the culprit. The hum of a hair dryer droned loudly. A door opened and then shut.

Monique heard herself say, "Which one of you wrote this on my locker?" Her voice quivered, as she fought for control, willing herself not to cry, not here, not in front of all these white girls.

Of the twenty or so women in the room, a lone giggle tauntingly resonated from the back of the room. Monique's eyes roamed to see where the cackle came from. It was the tall Russian blonde who looked like a man. She had large breasts that looked as stiff as boards and round like balloons.

Her name was Tatyana Fedorov. She was once the headliner of the show, that was until Monique Cheeks came along and took her spot, earning the stage name "Fire" because everyone said her show was hot.

Gingerly, Monique walked over to the middle of the dressing room floor as she studied the woman. Not only was she about ten years older than Monique, she was at least a full foot taller.

Monique spoke curtly, "You may not like me, but you're damn sure gonna have to respect me." Her tone was measured in an attempt to bridle her anger. "Just like most of you, I came here to feed my family, my child." Her voice cracked with emotion as her eyes rimmed with tears.

As her shoulders slumped, she suddenly thought to herself, Maybe this whole thing would just go away if I acted like the better woman and walked away.

She did what her mind told her, but as she did, Tatyana and her friends' stinging laughter filled the air. Automatically, Monique spun around and stared all three of them down.

"One of you bitches find something funny?" Monique pointed in the big Russian's direction as the girl stepped forward. She had narrow shoulders with long wiry arms. "Yes, you need to leave here … leave us … alone … go back to your watermelon and fried chicken," Tatyana spoke in broken English.

What disturbed Monique most was the pure hatred the woman carried in her eyes.

"Naw bitch, you need to leave me alone! You don't know who you fuckin' with!" Monique turned and walked away, but the women continued to laugh.

Monique was from Brooklyn. All the girls in her rough neighborhood had grown up fighting boys. It wasn't even an option.

Fighting back was a way of survival. Leisurely, Monique strode over to her locker with her mind on the matter at hand. The rest of the girls in the dressing room went back to what they were doing, gossiping and getting dressed.

Monique could hear the big Russian using the word "nigger" like it was standard everyday language for her and her pals. The sound of the word infuriated her. Never in her entire life had a person outside of her race called her a nigger.

With her back toward Tatyana and her clique, furtively, Monique opened a pack of razors, peeled one from the pack and placed it in her mouth. Quickly, she dressed in a white T-shirt, blue jeans and sneakers. She then reached for the Vaseline and put it on her face. At a demure 5 feet, 6 inches, she strolled over to the big Russian and her friends. "Which one of you bitches called me a nigger?" Monique asked tersely, while her brown eyes sized up the Russian.

Tatyana looked down at Monique and smirked devilishly as three other girls came and stood next to her. They made no secret of their attempt to jump on Monique. It was now six to one.

They began to surround her. One of the girls had something she was trying to conceal in her hand. Tentatively, Monique took a step back as her mind hurried to evaluate the situation. It was simple: she had fallen for the oldest trick in the book. Tatyana had set her up by taunting her to walk right into a trap.

Instantly, she looked over her shoulder for the door and realized that she was in great danger. Timidly, she took a step back. Even with the razor in her mouth she knew that it would be a difficult task to fight all the women.

They began to close in. "Nigger, what you gonna do now?"

Tatyana threatened. Doomed, Monique braced herself as they closed in on her.

"Uh-uh, it ain't gonna go down like that! Not today!"

Monique turned her head toward the sound of the voice. It was the white girl who casually spoke in passing. She elbowed her way through the crowd. In her hand she had a black can of mace and aimed it at Tatyana's face.

"I'll air this bitch out first before I let all y'all jump on this girl."

Fear showed in Tatyana's eyes as the rest of her girls stood back, intimidated. In that split second, perhaps it was fear, or just the willpower and desire not to be defeated, Monique seized the moment and lashed forward, striking Tatyana on her long beak nose, breaking it in three places. The rest of the girls quickly decided they didn't want none of Monique and got the hell out the way.

In a whirling blur of motion, Monique punched Tatyana like she was a man. It happened so fast. Monique then kicked Tatyana in the stomach. Tatyana screamed in agony as her tall, lithe body keeled over. Monique lassoed her fingers through Tatyana's long blond hair and yanked it hard as she brought her knee up to meet Tatyana's face. The bone collided with the soft tissue of her face.

The sound was like a baseball bat hitting wood. Blood squirted like a faucet as three teeth slid across the floor. Tatyana fell in a heap, face first on the floor.

The rest of the women in the room looked on in pure shock. Monique spit the razor out of her mouth, causing the girl that had come to her rescue to take a step back. Monique did a full circle in the room as she stood over the unconscious Tatyana lying at her feet, blood streaming from her face.

"Do the rest of you bitches want some of this nigger here?" She scanned the room, looking for a response.

The white girl who had come to her rescue smiled. As most of the girls scrambled to get away, one of Tatyana's friends rushed to her side and felt for a pulse. She immediately reached for her cell phone and dialed 911. As she requested an ambulance, Monique thought about what had just transpired. Not only was she sure she would lose her job, but even worse; she feared she might be arrested for assault. She left the scene in a hurry without even saying thank you to the white girl who had come to her aid.

The next night when she came to work, Monique was surprised to learn that management had learned of the incident and was shamed by it. To learn that racist epithets had been scrawled on Monique's locker and that it had caused an altercation was bad news. The kind of news that would not only be bad for publicity but it could have warranted all kinds of civil law suits for racial insensitivity.

To her utter surprise, Monique was given her own private dressing room. Also, management paid for Tatyana to have reconstructive surgery on her face. She was also given a handsome sum of money to drop any future lawsuits. However, Tatyana's beautiful face would never be the same. She was forced to find employment elsewhere.

Three days after the fight with Tatyana, an executive from "Gentlemen's Magazine" approached Monique. He had just so happened to be in town and had seen one of her shows. Although she was black, her beauty mesmerized him.

After the show, he approached Monique with a proposition. It was a long shot, but he was willing to try it if she was willing to invest a little time. He asked her if he could fly her to

California to do a photo session for the magazine. If the photo session went well, Monique would be offered a seven-figure contract to be a model and possibly a chance to be Model of the Year. Her picture would be viewed by millions of men all over the world. If worse came to worst, she would still be paid $2,000 for her time.

Monique was awestruck beyond words. After all, she was a twenty-one-year-old Brooklyn chick, still illegally receiving welfare checks.

Damn, white folks got it going on, she thought. Now her only problem was Rasheed, her baby's daddy. He would go berserk! For two months, she had been leaving him at her house, taking care of their three-year-old son, acting like she was working the midnight shift at the baker y. He never questioned her. God, he was going to be crushed when he found out she was a stripper.

The bad part was, she had no plans to stop working any time soon. And now, the offer to pose nude for Gentlemen's truly blew her mind. She fought with herself about how to tell him without breaking his heart. Then it dawned on her – there's no way a woman can tell her man that for the past two months she has been dancing nude as a stripper.

As she drove home that night to face Rasheed, she was determined to tell him about her deep, dark secret. She pulled into the parking lot of the rough, crime-ridden, drug-infested Marcus Garvey projects. If by some uncanny fate you lived there, you would be considered family. Unfortunately it was family of the worst kind. The family of shattered dreams and broken promises, where tomorrow never comes and the days are always too late.

Monique Cheeks was determined to find a way out, maybe even at the expense of leaving her man. Maybe?

She closed the door behind her as she walked into the sound of the TV blaring. Rasheed and baby Malcolm were asleep on the living room couch. One of Rasheed's long legs hung over the armrest. The two of them were beautiful together, father and son, as they slept.

Malcolm is the spitting image of his father, she thought as she peered down at her man and child. The moment was gentle as the two slept. For Monique, it was one of those Kodak moments.

Even in sleep, Rasheed's potent masculinity was vibrant and strong. Monique resisted the urge to stroke his cheek. Instead, she took off her shoes and placed her purse on the table. Roaches scattered in every direction. She decided to place her purse on the floor next to the couch.

Rasheed stirred in his sleep. She drew in a deep breath as she fought the urge to smother his handsome face with kisses. At 6 feet, 9 inches, she pictured him running up and down the basketball court. She thought about him, his dreams and his aspirations.

Although he would emphatically deny it, Rasheed loved basketball more than he loved life itself.

Rasheed Smith wanted to be a professional basketball player. He attended a small college, St. John's University, and for two years in a row, he had led the nation in scoring and assists. In his senior year of high school, all the major colleges recruited him;

however, that same year he got caught riding in a stolen car with drugs in it.

He was arrested and went to jail for a few months. The only reason he was released from jail and given a light sentence of probation was due to his high school coach, a man by the name of Dan Reeves. He and the judge were friends. Rasheed's arrest made headlines across the nation in the sports section and suddenly all of the major colleges that had expressed interest in him dropped his name from the list.

Rasheed was forced to attend a small college where every night he lit up the scoreboard with as many as fifty points a game. Sure, the NBA scouts were watching, but would they take a chance on a troubled black kid that had never known his mother or father?

His elderly grandmother had raised him as best she could, and many in the community felt she had done a good job.

With her hands clasped in front of her, Monique looked at the sleeping Rasheed as images flashed before her eyes – images of herself dancing nude. If only God would give her the courage to tell him so she could finally get it over with. Again, she wondered if he'd leave her or even worse, kick her ass.

She bit down on her bottom lip with a feeling of deep despair and guilt. She thought about the $2,700 she had in her purse; money she had made that night. Not only that, but she had $22,300 stashed in the closet in a shoebox. In less than a month she was scheduled to fly to California for a photo shoot for the magazine. If she passed the initial screening, the rewards would be many, the money would be huge, and the opportunities would be endless.

"Oh, baby, please don't be mad at me," she whispered in the dim light with her nerves on edge. This night she decided she was going to tell Rasheed and let the cards fall where they may.

Suddenly his eyes fluttered open. A beacon of light shined through the worn out curtains accentuating the brown flecks in his eyes. Rasheed reached up to grab her. Startled, she screamed. He laughed. Playfully she hit him on the chest as she fell onto the couch into his arms. They kissed passionately as the baby stirred in his sleep with his body now wedged between his parents.

"You scared me, musty breath." Monique wrinkled up her nose and playfully hit him on his chest again. He frowned, making a face as he looked at her.

"You smell like cigarette smoke," he replied.

"I … I … uh gave a girlfriend a ride home from work. She smoked in the car," Monique lied and changed the subject. "Did you miss me?"

"Yeah, I missed you," he said groggily.

"How much?"

"This much." Rasheed threw back the covers showing her his morning erection outlined in his boxer shorts.

"Wow, you could hurt a girl with that thang, daddy," Monique said flippantly and reached down to caress his penis ever so gently with long, even strokes.

"What time you gotta go to basketball practice?" she asked with a husky timbre of lust in her voice.

"Seven o'clock."

"We got time for a quickie?" She began kissing his neck below the earlobe.

"Only if you let me hit it from the back." He smiled sheepishly.

"Aw, you want a little doggy style," she chimed as she felt his hands fondling her breasts, unbuttoning her blouse.

With his forefinger and thumb he freed one of her breasts and leaned forward, taking it into his mouth and savoring the taste. She released a sigh, beckoning him to take her.

"Go put the baby in his bed … and you can have all the doggy style you want, sweetheart," she said, feeling her nipple harden with the sensation of his tongue.

As he attempted to get up to honor her request, she sucked in a deep breath and her tone changed. "I need to talk to you about something. Something I've been meaning to tell you for quite some time." She was determined to look him in his eyes.

Rasheed detected something in her demeanor that alerted him something was up. He rose up on his elbows with his brow knotted and looked her in the eye.

"Tell me what, Mo?" he asked suspiciously. She eased up off of him and walked over to the window. She could not bear seeing the hurt on his face for what she had to say next. She inhaled deeply.

She could feel her heart pounding in her chest so hard it felt like she was having trouble breathing.

"My job …" she said, trying to figure out how to start the conversation.

"Yeah," he said as he waited for her to speak again.

She turned toward the window searching for the words to say.

Rasheed immediately walked toward her and put his one free arm around her waist and pulled her into his body. "Baby, it'll be alright. We'll get through it," he reassured.

Rasheed thought she had lost her job. She knew this and his comforting words and gestures were making her admission harder.

"Baby … remember I told you I was working at the bakery?"

Rasheed didn't answer. "Well …" She made a face and swallowed the dry lump in her throat. Suddenly a gust of emotions overcame her. "I don't work there anymore." He held her with a blank stare.

"I've been dancing."

"Dancing?" he retorted. "What kind of dancing?" he asked, raising his voice so loud it made her flinch.

Monique wondered if he would hit her.

He stepped away from her, looking at her as if it was his first time really seeing her. For some reason his nearness was starting to make her feel uncomfortable; she wanted to run out of the house, but she had come too far to turn back now.

"I've been dancing at the Gentlemen's Club," she blurted out as if to get the evil words off her tongue.

"YOU WHAT!?" he bellowed angrily as he stepped a little closer to her, giving her a look of disbelief. "Tell me you're joking," he said, his brown eyes holding her captive.

Somberly, Monique shook her head slowly from left to right indicating she wasn't joking. She cast a long stare down at the floor refusing to meet his eyes. Her hands repeatedly washed over each other. She was a bundle of nerves.

"I've been working there for over two months now," she revealed, feeling a surge of emotions like a floodgate that was finally released. "I make more money in one night than I did for an entire month at the bakery."

"You're a fucking stripper? Is that what you're telling me?" Rasheed said indignantly, causing Monique to turn and glare at him. Frustrated, he mopped his face and raked his hands through his curly hair.

She had hurt him to the core of his being, as only a woman could. Monique wanted to hold him desperately, to assure him that all was going to be okay. "It's really not all that bad," she said softly. I dance for mostly rich older men."

"Mo, that makes it betta 'cause you dance for white men?" he shouted as he placed his feet firmly on the floor, giving her a look of disbelief.

The baby awakened and Rasheed sat back down on the couch, letting the baby crawl into his lap.

"What about your dreams?" He pointed at her. "Our dreams?"

He pointed at himself and their son. "Since the first day I met you, you talked about wanting to be a dancer. What happened, Mo? This the kind of dancin' you dreamed of?" he asked curtly with the strain of the situation showing on his face.

Something about the way he said that dug deep under her skin causing her to lash out with words.

"You think I wanna do this?" She peered at him. "Those were dreams, Rasheed, dreams! In the real world you got me pregnant at eighteen years old and that's when I learned that my dreams wouldn't put food on the table, or pay the bills." She looked around the apartment and saw a roach making its way into a crack in the wall. "I'm living here in this roach trap and you living with your grandmother. When was the last time you had a job, Rasheed? It's been over two years," she reminded him. "You got the nerve to talk about my dreams? What the hell am I supposed to do? Yo' ass ain't helpin' me none!" Her words hit him like a sledgehammer.

"Helpin' you none? Helpin' you none?" he yelled at her.

Innocently the baby looked on with those eyes, undecided if he wanted to cry or not. "Every day that I go to school I'm helpin' you. Ever y day that I step foot on the basketball court and an NBA scout comes out to watch, I'm helpin' you." And then, as if on his second wind, with a furrow in his brow he asked, "You don't believe in me no mo'?"

She didn't answer, but the cold expression on her face said enough. "You're gonna quit that fuckin' job and take yo' ass back to the bakery!"

"And suppose I don't want to? What you gonna do, make me?"

Her words were bold as she crossed her arms over her chest and narrowed her brown eyes at him in defiance.

Momentarily, he was stunned by her reply. Lost for words, he just stared at her with his lips pressed tightly together in an attempt to control his temperament. Then suddenly something washed over him causing his features to soften to the face of a defeated man.

"Mo … Mo, you my woman, not some freak show for other men to get their thang off. My woman …" He sat down and lowered his gaze to the floor. Like a broken man he asked, "Mo, why you doing this to me … to us?"

She heard the pensive tremor in his voice and saw how his bottom lip began to quiver. He was experiencing the pang of humiliation that a man experiences when he realizes his woman and his world are about to crumble down right before his eyes. His pain affected her in the worst way. She knew it was a man's bravado that would often not let them see past their egos. Right then she knew she needed to try a different approach, something more subtle.

"Listen, baby," she said with compassion, her voice terse and filled with intent. "Me and my child, we can't live like this."

Monique began to cry as she spoke barely above a whisper. "We gotta get out of here." She paused as she looked around the room, then continued, "This ain't livin. You're gonna have to put your pride and ego to the side." She looked at her purse. "Look, I have $2,700 in my purse and over $22,000 stashed in a shoe box in the closet." She stopped and mopped at her eyes with the palm of her hands. "Rasheed, baby, we got enough money to move outta here." Her voice was now a desperate plea.

He just looked at her and shrugged his shoulders. It was hard for her to read his thoughts.

Silence. They both just stared straight ahead as dawn started to creep through the window. She could hear the rustle of air as he sharply expelled a deep breath through his nose, as if he was fighting something deep within his soul. The moment lingered awkwardly with the still quietness of lovers who had found out they did not really know each other.

Monique wept. A stream of tears ran down her cheeks.

"Rasheed, I love you … but so help me God, if me and my child can escape from this hellhole then I fully intend to. Why do I have to live like this if I can help it? My mother was raised in these projects and so was I. I don't want my child to inherit this," she said, gesturing with her hand. Monique swallowed hard as she continued, "The other day at work I met a man, a white man, who is an executive at Gentlemen's. He's seen my show and wants to fly me to California for a photo shoot. If I pass I'll be in the magazine." Rasheed just looked at her with a blank stare. She continued, "I know it's a slim chance, but if I accept it, it would be the opportunity of a lifetime."

"Nude? They want to take pictures of you nude?" he asked, making a face at her.

She rolled her eyes up at the ceiling, giving him a look that might have said, "no dummy, they want me to pose in an Eskimo suit." She didn't answer his question.

The baby, now getting restless, lassoed his arms around his father's neck and for some reason both father and son turned and looked at her accusingly, with the same pair of hurt-filled eyes – two against one. She couldn't help but feel guilt-ridden as she watched Rasheed kiss their son on the forehead and whisper something into his ear. Slowly, he looked up at her. The dark circles under his eyes, along with his sulking face, told her his disposition.

His voice trembled as he spoke, "Mo, I could love you if you were fat, old and gray. I could love you if you worked at a bakery for the rest of your life. I could love you with my very last breath, 'cause a nigga love you to death," he said with a frown tugging at the corners of his mouth. Hurt was smoldering in his eyes like a dark volcano about to erupt. "But I can't love you if you selling your body by dancing nude, degrading yourself for the love of money." With that, his shoulders slumped. For the first time he was exposing a side of him that she had rarely seen before. "Love shouldn't have boundaries or limitations in the form of financial expectations. You're putting a price on our love. Please don't do this to us … to me, Mo."

"What part of this don't you understand?" she interjected with steel in her voice. "I'm not selling my body, nor am I trying to hurt you and your manly ego. We need the money. I couldn't care less about those men looking at my body. Hell, you even said it yourself, I have a beautiful body."

He narrowed his eyes at her, optic slants that could kill. Instantly she regretted what she had said, all the while she wondered how to get through his thick skull to his brain. Men!

"I'm not going for it," he said loudly. The baby began to cry as he reached for his shirt and grabbed his car keys off the table and headed for the door.

"Rasheed! Rasheed! Please don't go," she pleaded with her voice filled with the dread of losing her man.

Now she regretted even wanting to tell him, but in her heart and soul she knew that she had to—for the sake of her future and the opportunity at a ticket out of the ghetto. The problem now was, would she take it?

Rasheed turned around at the door. "I don't think I'm coming back," he said over his shoulder, not bothering to look her. "I need time to think about this."

"Think about what?" she volleyed in an attempt to stall him, hoping he wouldn't leave. She needed him to stay, not just now, but forever. She asked, "Are you going to watch your son tonight?"

He turned and looked at her long and hard. Finally he answered, "No," as he kissed Malcolm on his forehead and gently shoved him into her arms.

Malcolm immediately reached for Rasheed, which tugged at his heart. And then on second thought, he said, "Just bring the baby by my grandmother's house tonight."

With that he looked at her with bitterness in his eyes and walked outside, closing the door to their lives.

Seven

Jack and Gina

Gina drove the Lexus from the Galaxy Hotel. Palms sweaty, she steered the car slowly, weaving through the crowds of scattered police cars and foot patrolmen. An officer waved, signaling for her to turn his way. Gina ignored him. She could feel her heart pounding in her chest so hard that she felt nauseated. She gulped down air into her lungs as she tried to take deep breaths to soothe the urge.

The officer in the garage had ordered her to pull over to the side of the building so that she could give a description of the gunman. She drove to the corner even though the officer called for her to stop. All she could think about was Jack's last statement, if the police open this trunk I'm coming up blasting!

She was sure he meant what he said.

Making a left at the corner, a beautiful morning dawn stared her in the face as a pack of stray dogs roamed the street, crossing directly in front of the car causing her to pump the breaks, barely coming to a stop. She thought she heard something thump in the trunk causing her to gaze up at the rear view mirror.

She saw the bright lights of approaching police cars racing toward her. She pushed the pedal to the metal. The luxury car leapt forward, pulling away so fast that it threw her neck back. At a hundred and ten miles per hour she headed down one of Brooklyn's main thoroughfares, Linden Boulevard. The early morning streets were nearly deserted. The chase was on! Gina ran through all red lights as a caravan of police cars with flashing lights followed her in hot pursuit.

Up ahead to her right, she saw a speeding Amtrak train headed in the same direction as she.

She glanced in her rear view mirror again. The police cars were gaining on her with alarming speed. Suddenly Gina had an idea.

It was dangerous as hell. With a determined look scrawled on her face, she focused all her energy on the speeding train as she passed it.

The passengers gawked at her in horror as Gina zoomed by.

Up ahead was a train crossing, with its wooden red and white gates lowered, and a red light blinking a warning sign flashing: DO NOT ATTEMPT TO CROSS! Once she felt she had distanced herself enough from the train, she stepped on the brakes causing the car to go sliding … sliding … sliding, fishtailing, as she frantically fought for control. She came to a stop in front of the train's crossing section as it approached.

The speeding locomotive was only a few yards away with the police cars even closer, fully intent on ramming her car. Then she did the impossible. She punched the accelerator and plowed through the red and white wooden gates, shattering them into pieces as she drove in front of the oncoming train. Suicide?

After her death-defying escape she drove the short distance to Coney Island to a house that Jack had her rent under an alias. She parked the car in the garage. With her heart still racing, nerves on edge, she still could not believe she had pulled a stunt like that to get away. No wonder so many people got killed trying to outrun the police. The adrenaline rush along with the sheer desire to want to get away will make you do some crazy shit.

Gina walked out from the dark garage to see if the coast was clear. A light breeze played in her hair as the bright morning sun felt hot on her cheeks. To her surprise, she felt her body trembling as she looked in the sky and saw a police helicopter hovering at a safe distance. For some reason she laughed out loud and ducked back into the garage. With a feeling of exhilaration, she popped the trunk of the Lexus. Jack aimed the AK-47 at her head, ready to fire.

Damon Dice was still unconscious. He had a bleeding six-inch gash on his forehead. Jack hopped out the trunk. His clothes were soiled and dirty. Gina detected the rank smell of urine mixed with fear coming from the open trunk as she looked at Jack. Elated, she wanted to hold him.

"Bitch! What you tryna do? Get a nigga kilt?" Jack pulled the ski mask up over his face to reveal an angry expression which punctuated his wrath as he stepped toward her, causing the smile on Gina's face to freeze as she braced herself for the slap across her face she was sure would come.

"You were s'pose ta just walk away if anything went wrong!" He said angrily as he reached out and grabbed her by her throat, nearly cutting off all the air to her lungs.

She had never seen him this irate in her entire life. She just stood her ground, her nostrils flared and eyes bulging with a glint of defiance.

"Girl, I dunno what the fuck has gotten into you since I went away. You fuckin' crazy or some shit now? And where in the fuck you get that gun? Huh?" Jack screamed in her face as he began to choke her.

No answer. Her eyes began to fill with tears.

"Where did you get the fuckin' gun?" Jack asked again. "I thought I heard a fuckin' train when you was racin' up and down the street wit' me in the trunk. Girl, let me find out you was doing some dumb shit," he yelled as he looked at her face.

Still no answer. He watched her green eyes rim with tears. Then suddenly something about her unnerved him as he watched her delicate bottom lip tremor. She wasn't afraid. And not just that, Gina wasn't the little girl that he had left to let the streets raise while he was in prison.

Gina spoke calmly and directly, "If you think a bitch fitna run off and leave you, you got life fucked up." She spoke audaciously, completely taking Jack by surprise. "And if you wanna know the truth, it was you that taught me this lifestyle. You," she pointed at him, "showed me how to survive on the streets and then you went away." Gina began to cry in sobs that racked her body.

Jack released his grip on her throat and stared at her, stunned.

"You took me out the house. You made me the woman I am today."

They heard a moan and both turned and looked down into the trunk of the car. Damon Dice was starting to regain consciousness. Jack raised his eyebrows at her, a slight warning, as he leveled the gun in Damon's direction.

"When you left, you told me to use my body to juice niggas out their paper. I wasn't going to sell my pussy for no crumbs."

"I also told you to take your ass back to school. I didn't tell you to start robbing niggas."

"Well, regardless of what you say, this is how you taught me to survive. While you were in prison serving a life sentence I held you down to the utmost like a thoroughbred bitch is suppose ta. All the while, your so-called friends was tryna holla at me, saying you had a lifetime in the feds and you was never gettin' out."

Wrinkles creased in Jack's forehead as what she was saying started to soak into his brain.

Gina slid her eyes away from Jack as her hand absently rubbed at the red welt left on her neck from his grip. "I had to hustle my ass off to come up with the forty grand for your lawyers!"

As he looked at her he wondered how many men she had robbed to come up with that kind of cash. He thought about the diamond Rolex watch she had given him. Suddenly he squinted his eyes, frowning as she looked at him, and it dawned on him: Gina had indeed changed. It wasn't just that her body had blossomed and her features had become sharper, defining her femininity. It was her interior, her mind. She now possessed the great enigma that had baffled men since time immemorial—a woman's brain.

Just then, Damon Dice opened his eyes. Jack pulled the ski mask back down over his face.

"Get yo' punk ass out the trunk nigga," Jack ordered as Gina looked on. It was something about this gangster that she just loved. To watch Jack do his thing, for her, was a sight to behold.

Jack stripped Damon of all his jewelry and then his clothes. Completely naked, he made Damon lie on the gray, rusty, steel workstation in the garage. There were small pieces of wood chips all over the table as if someone had once used the table for wood crafting. With his palms up, shivering, Damon pleaded for his life like a man about to go to the gas chamber.

"Shut up nigga!" Jack ordered calmly as Gina looked on.

The dank garage suddenly turned deadly quiet as in the distance, a helicopter could be heard overhead. "Bitch-ass nigga, I'ma give you a betta chance than you gave me."

"Who … who are you?"

Jack's eyes squinted and he turned his head to the side. "Didn't I tell yo' punk ass to stop talkin'," he said through gritted teeth.

Damon nodded his head up and down like a frightened kid.

"I'ma give you two choices," Jack said as he held up two fingers. He continued slowly and methodically. "You niggas left me for dead, and in so many ways, I was. Now I've risen like Lazarus and it's time for you to pay your debt to not only me, but also to society. I want the first installment in blood. You think very carefully about what I'm about to ask you." Jack wet his lips with his tongue in anticipation of what he was going to say next. "Now, you can either give me an eyeball or your rat-ass snitch tongue. That's a better choice than you gave me."

Damon Dice began to cry, sobbing as he lay on the table naked pleading for his life. "I don't even know you. Please!"

"Nigga, save the rap. Court is back in session and the jury has reached its verdict. It's either an eyeball or your snitching-ass tongue. I ain't got all day." Jack looked over at Gina as she stood impassive, unmoved by all Damon's pathetic babbling and crying.

Why couldn't niggas just die like men? she thought to herself as she turned and walked away.

"Where you goin'?" Jack called behind her.

"To the bathroom to put on something more comfortable."

She continued to walk.

Jack turned back to face Damon. "Nigga, you don't know who I am?"

Damon shook his head "no" as he sniffled tears.

"I'm the nigga you took the stand on. The nigga you lied on.

Them crackas gave me a life sentence, but now I'm back! Your eyeball or your tongue?" Jack drawled and removed the ski mask.

Damon Dice pissed a small stream on the table once he saw Jack Lemon's face.

About thirty minutes later, Gina returned. Her mood was jubilant as if the earlier friction with Jack had never occurred. She bounced into the musty-smelling garage, ponytail swinging, hips swaying. She always made it a point to look sexy for her man, because if she didn't, she knew another woman would.

She now wore a number twenty-three throwback jersey and a pair of blue Enyce low cut coochie cutter jeans. In her right hand was a blunt filled with purple haze. In her other hand was a glass of Hennessy.

There was an oil slick on the dirty floor that almost caused her to slip as she walked through the door. A splinter of sunlight streamed through the dusty windows into the garage while Hot 97 blared from the car radio. The controversial host, Wendy

Williams, was on the air talking about gay rappers who act like they're gangsters.

Gina's "oh shit" startled Jack, causing him to turn around and

look at her. He had duct taped Damon's mouth shut as he lay on the ancient-looking workstation butt-ass naked. As she scanned his body, she could see that he was brutally beaten. The lower left side of his chest was caved in grimly, causing the broken bones to protrude, pushing the skin into what looked like a hellish, deformed contortion. Working her way toward his face, she saw his left eye partially dangling from the socket as blood oozed out.

Muffled guttural sounds escaped from Damon's taped mouth.

"Oh my god! Oh my god!" Gina exclaimed, horrified by the sight of Damon's body.

"Girl, get the fuck outta here!" Jack said with the bloody screwdriver in his hand that he had used to gouge out Damon's eye. On the floor was a bloody brick. Jack's clothes were spattered with blood all the way down to his Timbs.

"No." Jack turned and looked at her like she was crazy. "I wanna stay and watch," Gina confirmed with her eyes wide open as she staggered, slightly nauseated.

Suddenly she felt the urge to vomit. She took a long swig from the glass and frowned as the strong drink went down. That didn't help the nausea, so she took a deep pull off the blunt and passed it to Jack.

Plaintively, Damon moaned as his eye found hers. He pleaded for his life. Hesitantly, she looked over at Jack and wondered what could have happened to him in prison to make him want to cause someone so much pain and suffering. As he filled his lungs with purple haze, he handed the blunt back to Gina then gave Damon his undivided attention.

"Nigga, this gonna hurt me more than it's gonna hurt you. You got one good eye left, you tryna donate that muthafucka too?"

Jack threatened as sweat gleamed off his forehead. He bent down over Damon, placing the screwdriver under his good eye, tracing it. Gina looked in horror.

"I wanna know a few things from you," Jack said evenly as he pressed the screwdriver harder on his face, causing Damon to flinch uncontrollably. "First, I wanna know why you took the stand and lied on me? I also wanna know where your man G-Solo lives. And last …" Jack said, taking a deep breath as he wiped at the sweat from his brow with the back of his hand. "I wanna know who is overseeing you at the company with the seventy-five mil budget, and where you got all the cash stashed at, the dope money you was hustlin' wit'."

"What's that?" Gina asked, pointing.

From the sound of her voice Jack could tell she was still intimidated by the sight of Damon's battered body. Jack turned and looked at her, annoyed. She was talking about the contraption Jack had placed on Damon's head.

"It's called a vice," Jack answered as he turned the vice causing Damon to let out a muffled agonizing scream. Gingerly, Gina stepped closer, examining the nigga-rigged torture contraption. It looked like a solid steel clamp. Next to him, his jewelry was piled high, like maybe someone had robbed an

Egyptian mummy. As the horrid scene started to crystallize in Gina's mind, she felt a scream about to erupt in the pit of her gut. This was the real sordid world of a gangsta. Damon's eyeball lay on his cheek as blood poured slowly from the hole that was once its home.

On the radio, eerily, Biggie Smalls' song, "Ready to Die" played. Gina took another swig of the Henn as she willed herself not to vomit.

Jack snatched the duct tape off Damon's mouth, causing him to whine. "M … M … My eye," Damon groaned in agony.

"I got more where that came from." Jack nudged the eyeball with the screwdriver. "Now tell me, why did you take the stand and lie on me?"

"I … I … I had to. They made … me …" Damon croaked in agony.

"Listen nigga, the faster you talk, the faster we can get you to the morgue, oops, my bad dawg. I meant to say emergency room."

Jack made a face at Gina.

"The cop … Brooks …" Damon's voice was barely above a whisper. "Brooks … 40 … Vito …" Damon's words were not clear.

"You talkin' 'bout Captain Brooks from Manhattan and the rappers 40 and Vito? Was they all behind the set up?" Jack asked, agitated because none of it made any sense.

It was true them cats looked up to Jack, but 40 and Vito had major beef.

"No, Captain Brooks showed me a picture of you … said they needed to get you off the streets." Damon winced in pain.

Jack snapped, "Nigga, on everything God love, if you complain one more time about your punk-ass eye, I'ma pull the otha one out. Now finish!"

Damon swallowed hard. "Captain Brooks and the feds wanted you, 40 and Vito off the streets."

"What, me?" Jack said out loud, as if talking to himself.

"Too … many dudes was … coming up … missing. Your name was … out there …" Damon drawled.

Jack was caught off-guard. Brooks would have to be dealt with, but how was he going to get word to 40 and Vito before the feds spun their insidious web of corruption?

For the next fifteen minutes or so Damon told all, including info about a powerful man by the name of Michael Cobin. He was over at Tony Records and responsible for how the money was spent on DieHard Records. Jack made a mental note to pay Mr. Cobin a visit, too. The white man was the Don King of the rap music industry. He could make or break a career with a simple nod of his head. Mr. Cobin was also connected to the mob; that alone made him dangerous.

"Now tell me where all that dope money at. The money you used to start the record label," Jack asked as he looked at Damon closely.

He motioned for Gina to give him the blunt again. He took a long drag and blew the smoke in Damon's face.

"It's … it's … in the bank," Damon clamored painfully as Jack placed the screwdriver underneath his good eye caressing it as he talked.

"Nigga, you brought this shit on yourself. You didn't have to get on the witness stand and lie about me, saying I told you about a body."

"I … I … sorry," Damon whimpered, feeling the pressure of the screwdriver underneath his good eye. He didn't flinch when the ash from the blunt dropped on his forehead.

"Yeah, I'm sorry, too, sorry that our society is starting to breed a whole generation of niggas like you. Back in the day they had a code—keep your fuckin' mouth shut!" Jack yelled as a dribble of saliva slid from the corner of his crooked mouth.

Gina bit her nails as she looked on.

"When you go to work with them crackas you can never come back, 'cause they make rats outta niggas by sellin' they soul for another man's life. And you know what hurt? It was thousands of niggas doing life just like me and we were all there because of rats like you. Nigga, you didn't even know me from a can of paint and you took the stand on me," Jack said with a menacing scowl on his face.

"They … made … meee!" Damon screeched with the passion of a man that knew his time was coming to an end.

"Uncle Toms is what they called niggas like you back in the day. Niggas that sell out their race for their own personal gain."

"No … No … No …" Damon cried.

"Son, you betta tell me where dem chips is at or I'ma dress your punk ass up in a box and send you back to your mama." Jack applied more pressure on Damon's face with the screwdriver.

"You gotta believe me! All the money is in the bank!" Damon pleaded.

"Fuck dat nigga!" Jack hissed with his top lip snarled in disdain as he shoved the screwdriver into Damon's face with so much force that blood squirted nearly a foot in the air. Damon howled in pain.

Jack heard a loud thud. He turned around to see Gina sprawled on the floor. She had fainted and was lying on her back in a large oil stain. Awkwardly, one of her legs was underneath her as if it may have been broken. Her hands were extended at her sides like a bad impression of Jesus nailed to the cross. Jack shook his head.

Women. And she wanna be gangsta, he thought.

Turning his attention back to Damon, painfully Jack thought about the promise he had solemnly made to all his homies in the joint, his heroes, the cats that stood up like men and did their time—giving the ultimate sacrifice, their lives, rather than betray the street code of ethics. Men knew that snitching on a man was no different than committing genocide because you're not just killing the man, you're killing the family, too. Somebody's father, son, brother, or husband.

As Jack looked down at Damon, he knew that he must be made an example of, but he was also smart enough to realize that his feelings were much too involved. He had done more damage to Damon than he should have, but still the dying man refused to tell him where the money was stashed. Maybe Damon didn't have the money after all, but Jack knew that would be going against the grain.

All real hustlers had a stash spot. Even when they do get legit, it's in their blood – you never know when it'll be time to get ghost.

The problem was making them talk. Jack had long reasoned that that was the whole purpose behind kidnapping. Ironically, in a world where discrimination was prevalent, kidnapping crossed all barriers. Men, women, children of all races were fair game for the fine art of abduction.

Frustrated, Jack turned the handle on the vice, tightening it on Damon's skull causing him to scream loud enough to wake the dead; if not the dead, the neighbors for sure. The pain was so excruciating that Damon almost welcomed death.

Once again, Jack thought, why won't this nigga tell where that cheddar at?

Jack had damn near cracked Damon's skull, and he had lost a lot of blood.

Jack had recalled reading literature somewhere dealing with a Chinese technique of torture. It involved teeth and the very sensitive nerves at the root of each tooth that are connected to the brain. Jack knew that he had to think of something fast.

At the end of the workstation was a pair of old rusty pliers. He reached over and picked them up. Taking a long drag off the blunt he looked down at Damon as thick smoke smoldered, curling out of his nose.

Jack said mildly, "Open yo' mouth." Damon's one good eye stretched as wide as a silver dollar as he realized what Jack intended to do with the pliers.

"Ahh, uhm," Damon mumbled, clamping his bruised lips shut tightly, making a face to show he refused to open his mouth.

Jack turned the handle to the jaws of the vice on Damon's head, causing him to open his mouth to scream. Jack shoved the pliers inside his mouth grabbing teeth and gums, twisting and pulling— a crunching sound of teeth being torn away violently from the root.

"Nigga, where dat muthafuckin' money at?" Jack yelled as he teetered on the ball of his toes, yanking and pulling. Damon experienced more pain than he had ever felt race through his brain.

Finally, Jack yanked out two teeth matted with gory, blood-dripping gums that resembled a chunk of hamburger meat.

"Two down, thirty mo' to go," Jack chimed as he dropped the teeth on the floor, wiped his hands on his pant leg and prepared to go back into Damon's mouth. Damon choked and gagged as blood poured from his mouth. His lips moved, but no words came out. He was trying to speak as he drifted in and out of consciousness. Jack knew that sleep was the cousin to death.

"Mama's … house …" Damon muttered as he dreamed of his body at peace in a closed casket. He welcomed it.

"Nigga, what did you say?" Jack asked, leaning over, placing his ear near Damon's lips.

No answer.

Jack reached for the bloody pliers again, determined to make him talk.

"Stop! Stop!" Gina hollered. She was terrified as she wobbled while holding her stomach. "Baby, I think he's tryna tell you something."

"Well, I'm glad you finally woke the fuck up," Jack said sarcastically as he glared at her. She ignored him as she forced her eyes away from the horrific sight of Damon's bloodied body.

Damn, how much pain can one man take? His face was barely recognizable as blood poured from both his mouth and eye. The right side of his chest was now caved in from where Jack had beaten him with the brick. Simply said, it was just too much for her to bear.

"The money … is … at my … ma's …house," Damon whispered in a hoarse voice. The one secret that every hustler knew he was supposed to take to his grave. Jeopardizing the life of his mother, Damon began to cough and spasm. He was choking on his own blood. Gina frowned as she felt her knees about to buckle and she held onto the nearby table for support.

"That's mo' like it, nigga," Jack said with a smirk as he took a long pull off the blunt, rubbing his hands together anxiously.

It suddenly dawned on him why Damon had refused to tell where the money was—a man's love for his mother. Being the rat that he was, Damon had told on her, too, with no remorse.

To Gina, her brief exposure to the other side of the life of a real gangsta was something she would never forget. In the years to come, she would adopt Jack's style of torture, just like she had been emulating everything else about her man. However, what she didn't know was, under the dirty apple standards of kidnapping and holding them for ransom policy, Jack's demonstration of torture to make them tell was the soft version. Normally body parts were sent to the family members as evidence that they were dead serious about their money. So far, Jack had not cut off any body parts, at least not yet.

Damon spilled his guts. He told Jack about the money he had stashed at his mother's house. It was a little over a million dollars. Damon pleaded the best he could for Jack not to kill his mother.

Jack assured him he wouldn't, under one condition – Damon had to get on the phone and tell his mother that a woman was coming over to get the money. Damon agreed. He made the call on one of the many cellular phones that Jack had just for the occasion. The phone was stolen, so it couldn't be traced back to the caller.

To all their amazement, Damon was able to talk to his mother. Instantly his mother knew something was terribly wrong as her son gave her instructions to give the two duffel bags of money that were stashed in her basement to a woman that was coming to retrieve them. The entire time he spoke, his mother's intuition kicked in and like most mothers with a son in the game—she knew the territory. She was living proof of that. Her son had taken her out of the ghetto and placed her in a big house in the suburbs. She drove a Benz. She knew the risks of her son's lifestyle were great, but what she didn't know, as she held the phone with her hands trembling, was that it would be her last time ever speaking to her oldest child.

Gina put on a disguise – a blond wig, dark shades and a baseball cap – and walked up the street to catch a cab to go pick up the money. One thing was for certain, Damon's mom would never call the police unless she was sure that her son was in harm's way.

With the help of the cab driver, Gina lugged the money to the cab.

When Damon's mom asked about her son with tears in her eyes, Gina could not dare look the woman in her face as her mind flashed back to the horrific scene at the garage with Jack standing over Damon holding a bloodied screwdriver. *I'ma dress your punk-ass up and send you back home to you mama in a box*, she remembered him saying.

"Yes, ma'am, your son will be back home soon. He just had a hangover, told me to come," Gina lied, not bothering to look at the older woman.

After she had picked up the money, everything went as planned. Now came the really hard part – the takeover of DieHard Records.

They say one of the worst things you can do is lock a man up with him having nothing but time to think. Jack had carefully orchestrated an elaborate plan. Now all he had to do was focus on the key players: Michael Cobin and G-Solo. Jack knew that G-Solo would temporarily replace Damon Dice and that Cobin would be overseeing the operations of DieHard until they found a replacement. Jack needed to move fast on G-Solo. With all the helpful information he had gotten from Damon Dice, he went along and put his plan in motion. He was going to have to recruit Gina one last time for the most dangerous task of all.

Jack contemplated his plans as Damon lay on the workstation table looking like a human science project gone bad. His lips moved, gurgling blood, as he struggled to talk. Jack bent down, nearly placing his eye to his mouth.

"Don't … leave … me … like this … kill …me …" Damon pleaded plaintively in a dry hoarse voice as blood dripped from his ears.

The claw-like clamps of the vice grip on his head were so tight that it was slowly crushing his skull. As Damon begged to be killed, Jack furtively nodded his head with sympathy as he reached down to the floor retrieving a pair of shears used in lawn maintenance. The sharp instrument was for cutting through thick bush, but Jack had another purpose in mind.

"I'ma need one mo' thang from you," Jack said matter-of-factly, ignoring Damon's pleas for death. "I want your lyin'-ass tongue for a kind of souvenir, a special memento to send to the good Captain Brooks and the rest of them hot-ass niggas to let them know that us real gangstas is still runnin' shit."

"You … fuckin' crazy!" Damon spat between breaths.

"I know, I know," Jack said in a singsong voice, "and that's why I promise you, I'ma send a lot of niggas to join you."

With that, Jack turned the vice causing Damon to open his mouth for the last time. He violently shoved the shears into Damon's mouth in order to cut his tongue out.

Afterward, tired and bloody, Jack needed a handsaw and some garbage bags. He was determined to make a grand statement: Keep your fucking mouth shut!

Eight

Rasheed Smith

Rasheed drove an old, raggedy, brown '86 Ford Mercury. The passenger door was dented with rust spots underneath the paneling. He affectionately referred to his car as "The Batmobile" Disdainfully, his girl Monique called his hoopty a piece of raggedy-ass junk. For some reason, whenever she said it, it always struck his funny bone and gave him a good hearty laugh.

When they were in high school, Rasheed would pick her up from school during fourth period lunch. She would be embarrassed as hell to be seen getting into his raggedy car, but Rasheed was the captain of the basketball team. Tall and lanky with a mane of curly hair and dimples and skin the color of roasted peanuts, Rasheed Smith could have had any girl he wanted in high school. Even back then, scouts, along with the media, were coming to watch his games. Rasheed was gifted in all spor ts, but he chose basketball, regardless of whether or not basketball chose him.

At fifteen, he was already 6 foot 5 and growing. Every major college in the United States was trying to recruit him. One even offered his grandmother money. She flatly turned it down. She had earned her profession as a nurse the hard way—making it through college during the Jim Crow era of blatant racism and "whites only" signs. But in some ways that had made her stronger and she wouldn't expect anything less from her grandchild. Call it Black pride, but she was determined that Rasheed would stand on his own two legs and not be given benefits because he was a gifted athlete.

Rasheed drove away from practice with a heavy heart and dampened sprits. As usual, the media was there snapping away, taking pictures of him. Rasheed even noticed French Stuart, the NBA scout for the Chicago Bulls. The draft was less than two months away, but all Rasheed could think about was Monique dancing naked. That day, Rasheed was all thumbs. He couldn't catch a pass, his man kept beating him off the dribble and most of his shots were air balls. The one day that he needed to impress, he looked pathetic.

After practice, Coach Jones chewed his ass out and told him to meet him in his office. Hesitantly, Rasheed knocked on the coach's door. A voice from the other side summoned him.

The coach was a middle-aged man in his for ties. He had a cherubic face with deep aquamarine eyes that always appeared to smile at the corners. His neatly cut salt and pepper hair was starting to recede at the top. With a wave of his hand he gestured for Rasheed to take a seat at the front of his desk.

The coach was seated behind a large oak desk that looked like it dated back to the ancient civil war days. The desk was cluttered with papers and other items, including a coffee mug with the school's emblem on it. The coach cleared his throat as Rasheed removed a folder off the metal folding chair and sat down. He felt uncomfortable. The coach cleared his throat again and pulled in a deep breath like a man about to enter uncharted territory with words.

"Son, you know my job is to basically teach you the fundamentals of basketball, also the importance of team sports."

Rasheed nodded his head. The coach sighed audibly as he reeled back in his chair.

"Today you played like shit!" the coach said, raising his voice and pointing a finger at Rasheed. "Once you realize you have a gift, you enhance that gift. Not just that, you must make it a habit to practice like it's your work. These people invest millions of dollars in a person's athletic ability and you sho'll better be able to produce. Today may have been your last chance." The coach's voice was hard like steel. Rasheed's shoulders slumped as he dropped his head looking at the floor.

"I'm having family problems," Rasheed muttered.

"Kid, is it your grandma?" The coach asked with concern.

"Naw."

"Your son?" the coach asked with his brow raised.

Rasheed swallowed the lump in his throat and answered, "It's my girl. She started dancing naked."

"Whaaat! That's what you're all worried about?" The coach screeched as he stood with surprising quickness and walked around the desk to grab a handful of Rasheed's T-shirt.

"That's what this is all about? You're worried 'cause your girl is stripping? Let me tell you something and you better not ever forget this," the coach huffed, red-faced. "A woman will do anything in the world when it comes to taking care of her child," he said, looking at Rasheed as he released his hold on Rasheed's T-shirt.

"Listen son, you can't really blame her. Trust me when I say she could be doing something a whole lot worse, not to say that stripping isn't bad, but, if you want her to stop providing a livelihood for her child by dancing, you need to start earning some money. Get signed by the NBA and I promise you, if she loves you, she'll stop dancing. Other than that, self-preservation is the first law of nature."

"But not like that, coach," Rasheed said brokenly.

"Yes, like that, and that's why a man will never understand the ways of a woman. Don't even try it son, it will drive you crazy." The coach chuckled. "Just take what I have given you today and remember, the climate is right for change. You," he pointed at Rasheed, "just got to make it happen."

The two men just looked at each other before Coach Jones looked at the calendar on his desk. "We've got one more practice before the big game. You better show up. Your future depends on it." The coaches were like mentors and Coach Jones was no exception.

At least now Rasheed felt he had a solution—get drafted into the NBA. It was a lot easier said than done. Still, after he left the coach's office, all he could think about was the love of his life, Monique Cheeks. As he drove through traffic, he ruminated on her poignant words, "… and yo' ass ain't helpin' me none!"

Rasheed slapped the dashboard. "Shit!" He cursed as he thought about what the coach had said. He looked at his hands on the steering wheel, thought about all those white folks that came to watch him entertain them. Could what the coach said have been true?

Nine

It was such a beautiful day that Rasheed decided to drive to Coney Island. He knew an Arab-owned store that had a sale on ice-cold beer. As he stopped at a red light at a busy intersection, he gazed up at the sky. Terr y-cloth clouds lingered, contrasted by a hue of heavenly blue, the kind of picturesque splendor that makes a man wonder about the crafty architect of the universe. Of God?

As Rasheed sat at the light he was sure to keep one foot on the gas, manipulating the pedal and the other foot on the brake, or else his old hoopty would stall. A homeless person, a vagabond, pushed a shopping cart across the street. The old woman must have had on six coats and other articles of clothing. It was close to one hundred degrees in the sweltering heat.

Rasheed's old car sputtered and coughed. "Come on baby, don't you act up on me!" Rasheed muttered under his breath as he felt a ball of sweat running down his chest.

Hot weather and old cars make for bad days. Just then, he looked up into the sweltering heat to see what looked like a mirage walking across the street in front of his car. He blinked his eyes as the ardent sun partially blinded him. Rasheed cupped his hand over his forehead to shield the sun.

He could recognize that Brooklyn walk anywhere. It was more like a bounce from side to side, arms swaying, pants sagging, shoulders thrust forward, thug style, like a man on a mission. That was his best friend, crazy-ass Jack Lemon, but how? It couldn't be. Jack had a lifetime in the pen for a lot of bodies that were never discovered, but still he was convicted by other people's testimonies.

Rasheed blew the horn frantically and damn near scared Jack Lemon out of his skin, causing him to jump nearly a foot off the ground as he reached for the pistol at his side. The light turned green. Rasheed jumped out of the car and called his friend's name as he smiled broadly. A look of relief washed over Jack's face as he took his hand out of his pocket and flashed Rasheed a smile. They met each other in the middle of the street and rough neck hugged in a jovial dance as cars tooted their disapproval. Jack gave the car behind them the middle finger as Rasheed opened the car door for him since the passenger's door didn't open. Jack slid inside the car—just as the vehicle stalled at the light.

"Fuck!" Rasheed cursed, hitting the dashboard and making a face of a spoiled kid, causing Jack to erupt in laughter.

It's good to see my old friend again, Jack thought as he looked up to see a huge black man with a short-cropped afro and thick mustache. He had a stump of a cigar in his mouth. In his eyes shined the pure rage and pent-up hate which New York motorists are notorious for. The big man peered inside the car looking Jack directly in the eye.

"If you don't hurry up and move this piece of shit I'ma—" Jack pulled up his shirt and flashed the chrome-plated nine.

"Yo, son! Don't make me bust a cap in yo' fat ass over some stupid shit. Now fall back!"

The big man's eyes got as big as saucers. "I didn't mean any harm, sir," he shuddered in an humble tone. Quickly, he backpedaled, stumbled and nearly fell as he walked back to his black SUV.

Rasheed turned the ignition and the motor fired to life.

"Nigga, you still got this raggedy-ass car?" Jack chided his old friend in a poor attempt to play off what had just happened with the big man.

Rasheed pulled away from the red light, leaving a trail of gray smoke behind. Rasheed just shrugged his shoulders as he looked in the rear view mirror and made a turn at the corner. Jack didn't even have to tell him what to do—keep his eyes on that black SUV. They both watched the vehicle as it drove straight ahead.

Rasheed sighed in relief as he turned to Jack and smiled genuinely.

"Damn son, I didn't think I would ever see you again." Rasheed smiled and punched Jack in the shoulder. "When did you get out?"

"A few weeks ago," Jack said as he glanced in the passenger's mirror.

"Damn, and you didn't holla at my fam?" Rasheed questioned with a frown. He was barely able to contain his disappointment as he glanced over at Jack and saw what looked like blood on his pants and Timbs.

"You know a nigga got mad love for ya, but you know how the streets is with all these niggas tellin' now-a-days. Niggas find out I'm back and they get larcenous 'cause they know my resume is impeccable for putting in work in this town. This time I'm on the element of surprise-type shit."

Rasheed understood, nodded his head and made a left at the corner.

"Man, it's good to see you. I still can't believe this." Rasheed beamed with joy and then added, "I'm about to enter the NBA draft."

"Get the fuck outta here," Jack gidded.

"No shit." Rasheed smiled proudly.

"You got an agent?"

Rasheed made a face as he shook his head "no".

"I'ma buy you an agent. What's that waterhead dude name …ah … ah …" Jack thought for a few seconds. "David Stern!" he said and snapped his fingers. Rasheed cracked up in laughter.

"Man, David Stern is the Commissioner of the NBA."

"What the fuck ever. You just as good as Kobe. You just need a shot at the pros."

"Yeah, me and about a million other brothas," Rasheed acknowledged as he hit the brakes to avoid hitting some kids who ran into the street. The car stopped at a red light. Jack peered over at the gas gauge.

"Damn son! You driving 'round on fumes in this bucket."

Rasheed ignored him as the car started to shake and sputter. A chocolate sista with generous curves strutted by pushing a baby stroller. She wore a floral sundress with laced shoulder straps. She made eye contact with Rasheed and smiled. Both men watched the sensuous sway of her hips as her plump behind moved from side to side.

"Yo, son, shorty lookin' for a baby daddy. With an ass like that she won't have to look too hard." Jack waved at the young woman.

She waved back, smiling like she knew him. The two old friends erupted in laughter as Rasheed pulled away from the red light.

Moments later, as they rode, Rasheed turned to Jack and asked, "Where you headed?"

"To the hardware store to pick up a few items."

"Items like what?"

"A handsaw, cement and some garbage bags."

Rasheed turned and looked at his friend just as an ambulance raced by, startling both of them. High in the celestial sky, a Goodyear blimp sailed by. Jack smelled burning oil and wondered how Rasheed could ride around in a raggedy-ass car like this. But it touched him as he thought about his best friend's loyalty.

"Yo, B, I got the magazines and all the articles you sent to me on your scoring titles. Oh, and thanks for the chips you sent me, too."

Embarrassed, Rasheed felt his cheeks flush. The most money that he could ever send was twenty dollars at a time.

Jack read his best friend's thoughts. "Listen my nigga, don't ever get it twisted. You and my shorty Gina was the only muthafuckas that held me down. I got mad love fo' y'all. It's cats in the joint that don't get no mail, no one comes to visit them, people won't even accept a phone call, basically they don't get no love. When you sent me those twenty dollars with pictures of your shorty and the baby, that shit touched me right here, B," Jack said, pounding his chest with his fist so hard it sounded like a bass drum. "You'd have to experience the shit to know what I'm sayin'. Shit was crazy. They had niggas packed in cells the size of a small closet, while up the street they had animal activists picketing at the zoo, talking about cruelty toward animals 'cause the gorilla's space was not big enough. Should have been cruelty against niggas. Cats in there serving life for twenty dollars' worth of dope." Jack made a face as he shook his head like he was reliving a bad moment in his mind.

Rasheed parked the car in the Ace Hardware store parking lot. The humidity was so high that you could see the heat vapors rising from the scorched concrete. A youngster with neatly French braided hair, dressed in an orange apron with Ace Hardware stenciled across it, raced by as he collected shopping carts.

Rasheed turned off the ignition. The old car sputtered as the engine continued to run. Jack snickered, "Damn son, you want me to get out and shoot this muthafucka?"

Rasheed peered over at him, his mind elsewhere. Finally, the car turned off.

With a serious expression on his face, Rasheed spoke. "What was it like in there?"

Jack turned his head away from Rasheed as he gazed out the window. "Death before dishonor is dead. It's legalized slavery now. One nigga get popped by the feds, he tell on twenty other niggas, most of them he don't even know. The judge told me in the courtroom, if I didn't cooperate he was going to give me life. That old cracka did just that when an all-white jury convicted me of five homicides where they never found any bodies."

"How did you beat the case?" Rasheed asked.

"Gina got me a lawyer. I beat it on appeal. They arrested me with an illegal search warrant."

"It figures," Rasheed huffed.

"They got factories in all the federal prisons," Jack continued. "The judges have investments in the factories like some kind of stock. They give niggas these big-ass fines that they know they can't pay and send them to work in the factory. Dudes working twenty-four-hour days, making less than four dollars."

"Damn, why won't the public or the people that can do something about it, do something?" Rasheed asked innocently.

"I dunno. Niggas on some bling-bling time and all the churches is exploiting so much money. Shit, in prison, ninety percent of rats claim to be Christians. Sayin' Jesus told them to go back and testify and shit. Don't care who they tell on."

"Get the fuck outta here," Rasheed said as he opened the door to let some fresh air in.

"One thing I did learn in prison, religion and the so called 'Holy Bible' are the biggest brainwashing tools on the earth. Fuck, was we heathens in Africa before they brought us over here and gave us Christianity? Teaching that bullshit about you gotta die to go to heaven where the streets is paved with gold. If that was true them crackas would be lined up killin' each other just to get there. Instead, they lined up killin' us, sending us to mythical heaven, while they enjoy themselves right here on earth." Rasheed raised his eyebrow like he wanted to say something. "A white man's heaven is a black man's hell."

"Man, you know I'm a Christian," Rasheed said, disturbed.

Jack retorted, "Nigga, you the one who asked me what prison was like."

Just then, a beautiful butterfly with an array of pastel colors – purple, blue and yellow – flew into the car. With surprising quickness Jack smashed it with the heel of his hand against the windshield. Startled, Rasheed looked at the wounded butterfly as its wings still fluttered.

"Did you know that 'God' spelled backward is 'dog,' and that we all are gods in our own way? If need be, a nigga cross me, I could kill another man just like I killed that bug," Jack said ominously, causing Rasheed to shudder.

As he looked at his best friend, it dawned on him that Jack had indeed changed. He wondered what could have happened to him to make him adopt such a mentality.

"Did you know that Jesus was a black man, a revolutionary? And that white men, the Romans, killed him 'cause they said he conspired against them? Just like they killin' niggas in the joint now-a-days and charging them with conspiracy. In John, Chapter 10 of your Christian Bible it says, 'Ye are gods.' Jesus said that when the Jews were getting ready to stone him for blasphemy, for claiming he was God."

"Man, you trippin'. You done let that place get inside your head," Rasheed said.

"Son, we all got God-type qualities in us. We just gotta find them. Ain't nothing wrong with religion, especially Christianity, but it has to be practiced from a black perspective."

"Why is that?" Rasheed asked, wishing he had never asked the initial question.

"'Cause the people in the Bible was black, and they don't want you to know that. That's why crackas use fear and God in religion, all in one."

"Man, what the hell does fear and religion got to do with you being God?" Rasheed questioned, with his brow knotted in frustration.

Jack sighed audibly as he placed his foot on the dashboard, giving his friend a weary look like, "you just don't get it."

"Peep game, playa. All this religious shit started out of Egypt. The Bible is only six thousand years old. Egypt is in Africa. It's over hundreds of thousands of years old—"

Rasheed interrupted, "Damn nigga, what you is, a historian now?"

Jack glowered at him with a face that said 'don't disturb me.'

"Naw, I'm no fuckin' historian. I just read a lot while I was in the joint. It's true what the crackas say about us. If you wanna hide something, put it in a book."

"I hope you read something other than history books 'cause you 'bout ready to start selling bean pies," Rasheed joked in a bad attempt to ease the tension that Jack created with his new farfetched prison theories.

"Yeah, I remember this one book I read where some lame was quoting Machiavelli. Don't get me wrong, he was a sharp cat, but niggas read that shit and took it literally. He said, 'It is better to be feared than loved. Fear you can control, love you can't.' That's some straight bullshit! There's a lot of good niggas in the joint with six-number release dates. Son, don't never forget this, real niggas don't deal in emotions. Period! Neither fear, nor love, because fear is what started witness protection. Fear is what makes good niggas go bad, flip the script, turn snitch on they men," Jack said vehemently, his face full of anger.

As Rasheed looked at him he was now certain that Jack had spent too much time in the joint.

"Son, I left a lot of good niggas in the joint. I know you ain't feelin' me on this. You probably think a nigga crazy buggin', but just ask Boy George and McGriff and all them niggas that was down with the Preacher Man Crew what fear will do to a nigga when them crackas start talking 'bout a lifetime in the joint or tell. See, like I was sayin', fear, religion and God are all used the same."

"Man, I don't know!" Rasheed said, throwing up his hands. "Y'all cats go to the joint, read a few books and become chain gang scholars or some shit."

A Mexican woman walked by. She glanced in the car and held her purse tightly as she picked up her pace.

"I'm just tryna raise my seed, be a man, do the right thing," Rasheed confessed somberly.

A yellow school bus passed slowly with children playfully laughing and screaming out the windows. Jack smiled dreamily and pointed at the bus. A beautiful little black girl with two ponytails, hair parted down the middle, frantically waved at them.

"That's our future right there. Them babies. I'm willing to die for what I believe in. Son, shit gotta change. We gotta star t being self-sufficient and independent. We need to start running all them Arabs and Chinese stores out our communities."

"Jack, you buggin' for real now."

"No I ain't. Shit, they don't spend no money in our stores, nor will they let you put a store in they hood 'cause they smart enough to know betta."

Rasheed felt his heart skip a beat as his eyes roamed down Jack's pant legs. Once again he wondered about the blood and was tempted to ask. Instead, he used another tactic.

"What do you think about brothas killin' brothas?" Rasheed asked as he glanced at the butterfly on the windshield. It had stopped moving.

Jack fanned hot air with his hand as he considered the thought. "This is how it works in the so-called American diplomatic society. You got the rich and the po'. Well, the rich, they steal from everybody and the po', we steal from each other, but that shit fitna change. All these modern day Uncle Tom-ass niggas is going to be dealt with. Back in the day they had a code of ethics– keep yo' muthafuckin' mouth shut and give somethin' back to the hood or else get a vicious beat down, and the next time you fuck up they leave you leakin'."

"Why you wanna kill black folks?" Rasheed interrupted, barely able to contain his distress over his friend's state of mind.

"'Cause we can't keep blaming this shit on the crackas when niggas is gettin' millions of dollars now-a-days and ain't investing it in our children's futures."

"You can't change that," Rasheed countered. "Niggas like to dress and buy fancy cars." Rasheed glanced over at Jack. He had his eyes closed as if in a trance. When he opened his mouth to speak it was eerie.

"Sometimes … sometimes when I close my eyes I hear voices, see faces, a river of blood, screams." As Rasheed looked at Jack, a tiny drop of sweat glistened as it cascaded down his forehead onto the bridge of his nose and teetered there. "I …

hear my father's voice." Jack's lower lip trembled as he frowned, reliving the moment in the dark crevice of his mind.

It was 1975. Jack Lemon was a small child. He and his dad had stopped by the Black Panther branch in Harlem, where his father was a member. They intended to spend some quality time together that day. They had only stopped at the Harlem branch to take some food to the brothas and sistas. Jack's father was the Minister of Defense for that particular Panther branch. It was a festive occasion. Jack had on his black beret like all the Black Panthers were wearing at the time. Barely able to look over the pool table, Jack ran, enjoying himself with the rest of the children.

As was typical, most of the Panther members were barely in their twenties. However, that never stopped them from debating about politics and laws that affected their plight as a people.

The James Brown song, "Say It Loud—I'm Black and I'm Proud," played while the young adults debated and the children ran and played. There was a loud knock at the door. Suddenly, the music died and panic-filled voices could be heard outside where the police lined the streets in full force. The entire street had been surrounded as people gawked out their windows, waiting for the drama to unfold. It was the police against the Black Panthers.

"Come out with your hands up and no one will be harmed," the police demanded from a loudspeaker. Jack Lemon's father, known as Big Jack, went to the door and opened it wide enough for the police to see that he was unarmed.

"Pig, if you have a warrant to arrest any one of us, let me see it. If not, you're in violation of our constitutional rights."

"YOU! Black male standing in the doorway! Disrobe and come out with your hands in the air where we can see them! This will be your last warning," the officer bellowed orders.

As the police spoke, inside the Black Panther's headquarters, members armed themselves in preparation to go to war. Young men and women determined to live or die for their human rights and to be treated as the Constitution of the United States says. Besides, they really knew what the police were doing. This was an old police tactic used to humiliate and harass blacks. The same tactic was being deployed all over the United States to eliminate all pro-Black movements that the government deemed a threat because young blacks had started resisting police brutality and other forms of oppression.

Lil' Jack watched his dad as the moment lulled with suspense, his eyes barely above the pool table. As Jack spoke to the police, a pretty pecan-colored woman with a big Afro stood guard as she had been trained.

"Pig, we got women and children in here. We ain't lookin' for no trouble. If you got a warrant that says we're in violation of any of your laws we'll honor that, but—"

POW!

A single shot rang out. Jack watched as his father keeled over in what looked like slow motion. The blood poured from the gaping hole in his neck. His father's dark sunglasses caromed off the wall across the room.

The sista with the big Afro opened fire in self-defense as she screamed at the top of her lungs, "Die muthafucka, die!" With marksmanship skill, she killed two officers. Soon a fusillade of shots rang out.

After an eight-hour gun battle with the authorities, the National Guard had to be called in. Twenty-seven Black Panthers massacred – men, women and children. The woman with the big Afro was a revolutionary by the name of Adia Shakur. She placed Lil' Jack inside of a metal cabinet, saving his life. Somehow she escaped. They were the sole survivors. To that day the government had a million dollar bounty out on her head, dead or alive.

Jack opened his eyes. "Sometimes … I see my father's blood. I know y'all think I'm crazy, but have you ever seen a product of its environment? It looks like me."

"So, I guess you must be on some revolutionary time now, huh?"

"Whatever." Jack smacked his lips. "All I know is muthafuckas gonna start dying."

"Have you seen Damon Dice yet?" Rasheed asked.

"Naw, I ain't seen dude," Jack lied as he peered at Rasheed, eyes full of mischief. "But in due time, I'm sure he'll pop up some place."

"What did he say against you at your trial?"

"Nothing that an eye and a tongue couldn't pay fo'," Jack responded.

"Huh?" Rasheed muttered, confused.

"Listen, I'ma keep it gangsta wit' 'cha 'cause I fucks wit' 'cha like dat. I just hit a lick on some shit that I've been plotting for years. And you know what, it feels good! Wasn't it Tupac that said that revenge is sweeter than pussy?"

Rasheed raised his brow at Jack.

"Son," Jack lowered his voice to a conspiratorial tone as he leaned toward him. "Shit fitna get hectic. Niggas gonna start dying. I caught a nigga slippin', so I gripped. Know what I mean? I'ma bring the pain in the worst way and the residue … well …" Jack had a menacing grimace on his face. "You just stand the fuck back and let me do me."

"Shit, man. You know that I got your back," Rasheed replied.

"Naw, you just stay in school and let me do my thang." He patted Rasheed on the back. "I made my first mil today and it's more where that came from."

"What?"

"Yup, and it was as easy as pulling teeth." Jack added his own personal humor as he thought about how he had punished dude.

"Tomorrow I'm gonna stop by your grandma's and we going shoppin' for a new whip for you." He looked at Rasheed's ride and continued, "Son, you gotta get rid of this ancient-ass bucket."

Rasheed gave his friend a quick once-over, like maybe he had doubts about Jack's tale of newly found riches. Once again he swept his eyes over Jack's gear. Jack picked up on his thoughts.

"Nigga, don't let my appearance fool ya! These my work clothes. Chuck-a-nigga-in-the-trunk clothes. Ain't much changed. I'm still dressing niggas in cement shoes, sendin' them back to they maker if they don't break bread. No mo' crumbs this time 'cause I got a Brooklyn crew of niggas that hungry, know what I mean?" Jack drawled.

"Shit done changed a lot since you been gone, Jack. Them cats got big bodyguards."

"Gina been sayin' the same shit about 'shit done changed'. Shit, as long as niggas still bleed like me, ain't a damn thang changed," Jack said and winked his eye as he took his foot off the dashboard. He then reached into his pocket and retrieved a large wad of cash. Rasheed's jaw dropped as he looked at all the money.

Jack peeled off five one-hundred dollar bills and extended his hand. "Here, give this to Monique." All Rasheed could do was smile.

Afterward, Rasheed dropped Jack off at an old, dilapidated house and watched Jack's Brooklyn gait as he bounced, shopping bags swinging from side to side with his determined strides.

As Rasheed drove away, for some reason his mind drifted back to Monique. The confrontation was inevitable. She was scheduled to pick up the baby that night at his grandmother's house.

Rasheed felt the five hundred dollars in his pocket and thought about her posing nude for the magazine and all the money that it could bring. He was forced to admit, the money sounded tempting.

Ten

The Gentlemen's Club

In Brooklyn, the wind moaned outside like a million pipes playing as the air gusted against the window panes. Monique Cheeks sat in her dressing room chair looking at herself in the mirror. She was clad only in her lace panties and bra. An old school R. Kelly CD played from the other side of the room. As she stared at herself in the mirror, she brought a delicate hand to her face, tracing her cheek and the bags that were starting to form under her eyes. She felt she was too young for this stress. For the past month, self-doubt and despair had consumed her. Outside her window, gaudy lightning ricocheted across the sky as torrential rains flooded the city.

Today had been one of them days, she realized as her mind reflected back to Rasheed. She didn't mean to hurt him the way she did. After she got off work she was scheduled to meet him at his grandmother's house to discuss their future, or perhaps their break up. Rasheed was all the man that she could ever want—the only man that she had shared her body with, the only man that she had ever loved.

Her eyes got teary as she stared at her crestfallen face in the mirror. She thought about Malcolm, their three-year-old son. He was the spitting image of his father. The last time she took him to the bathroom, Malcolm urinated all over the toilet seat as he tried to shake his wee-wee, emulating his father. Monique smiled through her teary eyes, then the smile waned, turning upsidedown as she thought about Rasheed. It caused her heart to pound in her chest. If he would only just let her dance one more month she felt they would have enough money to move into a nice neighborhood, and she could go back to college. She knew the photo shoot for the magazine was a long shot, like Rasheed's dream of entering the pros. Hell, he had a better chance than she did. But still Rasheed was being stubborn and too damn unreasonable. She made a face in the mirror.

"Rasheed!" she screamed at the mirror.

Just then she heard the loud roar of applause as a wave of clamor rose. The noise, the applause, continued for so long Monique had to go take a peek to see who the competition was getting all the noise on her stage. She threw on her robe and hurried out to catch the show.

To her utter surprise, the place was jam-packed. Monique wasn't the only dancer to come out from the dressing room. All the other girls had come up to find out what the loud commotion was all about as well. The women, like everybody else in the club, gawked at the stage in awe of the performance. Monique had to stand on her tiptoes just to get a view of the show. On stage a beautiful array of colorful lights flashed as G-Unit's "Magic Stick" played. It was Monique's first time ever hearing rap music played in the club and the lighting was new, too.

What she saw on stage blew her mind. It was the white girl who had come to her rescue when Tatyana and her girls set her up to get jumped. The white girl had an audacious body like a thick black woman with butt for days. Monique was rattled because she still couldn't recall the girl's name. On stage, nude, except for a silver and black glittery thong, her nimble body was deep copper toned, covered with a filigree of silvery sparkles. She walked on her hands, adroitly displaying the skillful acrobatics of a talented gymnast, as she approached the pole in the center of the stage. With her thick, brawny thighs she used her buttock muscles as she spun on the heel of one hand grabbing the pole with the mounds of her succulent butt cheeks, causing a ripple of gasps to erupt throughout the audience.

Everyone was astounded, including Monique, as she watched the white girl steal her show. While still on her hands, she did a scissor move spreading her legs wide, the lips of her vagina displayed like crown jewels in the luminous stage light as she made her butt bounce doing upside down push-ups on the pole – something that required enormous strength and agility. Then, she gracefully wrapped her long legs around the pole. In suspended animation, she removed her hands from the floor and raised, using only her legs, until her body was in an upright position. Then she spread her legs, grinding her crotch against the pole as she slid down. The lights went dim and the audience went wild. Even Monique was forced to applaud. Money was tossed at the stage.

Suddenly there was a loud clap of thunder and the lights went out, along with the music. The normally passive crowd started to get rowdy. The emergency lights came on. The tempestuous weather had knocked out the electricity, forcing the rest of the performances to be cancelled for the night.

Monique walked back to her dressing room in a funk. The canceling of the show meant she would make no money.

"Damnit!" She couldn't get the awesome stage show out of her mind.

What is that girl's name? she pondered as she walked back into her dressing room and closed the door behind her. "Georgia Mae? Yeah, that's it," she said out loud.

What kind of crazy ass name is that? she thought as she began to dress.

Everyone called her "Game" for short, and she understood why. The few times Monique had spoken to Game were only in passing and she had wanted to go to a black club and meet some brothas. She must have made it because she could dance her ass off. Monique had never seen a performance like that before; and not just that either, Game had a body like a sista with one of them big round ghetto booties.

There was a knock at Monique's door followed by a loud clap of seismic thunder that made her flinch. The lights blinked causing R. Kelly to skip a note on the CD player. She plodded to the door, now fully dressed, opening it. To her surprise the white girl, Game, stood outside. Monique smiled as she invited her in.

Game's blond shoulder-length hair was cut short in the front into ringlets that stylishly hung above her eyebrows. She had a beautiful oval face with enchanting green eyes.

"Fire, I need to talk you about something," Georgia Mae said, calling Monique by her stage name.

Monique twisted her lips to the side of her face as she said, "Girl, I know you ain't come in here on this messed up night to ask me about taking you to some black club so you can meet some men." The two of them giggled.

In some ways the two women were compatible. They were both considered outcasts. Mostly, it was by choice. Just as Monique had started disassociating herself from the rest of the women who worked at the club, so had Georgia Mae. There was just something about her that Monique couldn't put her finger on. Georgia Mae was sophisticated and she dressed real fly in all the latest designer clothes. However, when it came to picking men, she really didn't have a choice. Black men chose her because of her freaky round behind, shapely curves, taut waistline and large breasts. At 5 foot 9, she was considered a brick house that could give any black woman a run for her money.

Georgia Mae wasn't all body; she had ample brains. She graduated from Harvard with a 3.97 GPA. She had a Jurist Doctorate in Law and a Ph.D. in Psychology. Since the age of three, her mother had entered her in every beauty pageant and talent show she could find. It was as if her mother were trying to relive her failed beauty pageant years through her child.

At the age of eighteen, Georgia Mae Hargrove entered the Miss USA Pageant. She came in a disappointing third place. Her mother felt she knew why she didn't win. It was because her daughter did not have the physique like most of the white women she was in competition with. However, her physique mimicked those of the few black women that were chosen as finalists, and truth be told, Miss USA wasn't ready for a white woman with a black woman's body. Georgia Mae had enough when her mother suggested she have a surger y to reduce the size of her behind. Instead of concentrating on her physical assets, she decided to develop herself mentally and she enrolled in college. That was also the time the dancing bug bit her.

In college she met a smooth brotha by the name of Ozzie King, known to his friends as Big O. One day as she lay on the campus grass reading a book, he walked up and sat down beside her and made a comment about the book she was reading. She instantly found him strikingly handsome and intelligent, not to mention funny. Two weeks later he stole her virginity along with her heart. He introduced her to the world of strip club dancing, rap videos and eventually cocaine. All of Georgia Mae's life she had secretly been attracted to black men. It wasn't just black men, it was the culture – the music, the food, the dance, the style and most definitely, the sex.

On the other hand, it seemed like white men shunned her because of her curvaceous figure, one that they would expect on a black woman. Monique scanned Georgia Mae and saw that she was dressed sexy and provocatively in a cream-colored Baby Phat jacket with matching jeans. Underneath she wore a vanilla lace see-through blouse that highlighted her double-D breasts, along with her diamond navel ring and heart-shaped tattoo. Her feminine high-heeled Timberland boots seemed to accentuate her long bowlegs, exposing an eye-opening sensuous gap between her thighs.

As Monique took in the shapely curves of the white girl she couldn't help but feel attracted to her in some way, and for a fleeting moment, she wondered if she could be gay. She quickly flung the stupid idea out of her mind. Georgia Mae was just one of them rare crazy-sexy-cool white chicks that could comfortably blend right in with the sistas.

As Monique looked at Georgia Mae she noticed her damp hair, fringed at the ends like she had just gotten out of the shower. Once again, Monique thought of the several occasions she had hinted at going out partying together. She was half-expecting her to ask again as she gazed up at her, but for some uncanny reason, images of the stage show flashed in Monique's mind. She couldn't help but ask, "Georgia Mae, girl, where did 'ja learn how to pop your coochie like that?"

The white girl smiled brightly. "Ever since I was a little girl my mother had me entering mostly black talent shows because she said black folks had natural soul and that made them the best in the world at singin' and dancin'. She said if I could compete with them I could compete with anybody."

"Did you win any?" Monique asked out of curiosity.

Georgia Mae made a face and answered, "I lost more than I won, but at seven years old, growing up around black kids was a positive experience for me." For the first time Monique noticed the beauty mark above her right cheek as Georgia Mae continued to talk.

"My mother said that Elvis Presley used to sneak backstage and watch the blacks perform. He would steal all their routines. That's how he got so famous."

"Did your mama tell you that Elvis said that all a nigger could do for him was kiss his ass and shine his shoes?"

Georgia Mae raised her brow at Monique causing her to instantly feel bad about letting that roll off of her tongue.

Suddenly, the elements outside made a mighty rumble, causing both women to shudder.

Silence.

Monique turned and tensely glanced out the window.

"Uh … anyway, for some reason the black girls at the talent shows nicknamed me 'Game.' I thought it was kind of cool, so it's stuck with me ever since."

Monique nodded her head in agreement. "I never would have thought your name would be Georgia Mae."

"Me neither," she laughed. "When I was born, my daddy showed up at the hospital drunk and unmanageable. He's a very big man; actually he's a damn fool when he's drunk. That was the first name that came outta his mouth after I was born. My mother wasn't one to argue with him while he was drunk, so Georgia Mae he said, and Georgia Mae it was."

Monique got a good laugh out of that as she turned away from the window and the pouring rain. She saw cash stuffed in Game's Gucci handbag. It painfully reminded her of the money she was going to miss due to the storm outside. She couldn't help but wonder, with all Game's education and talent, not to mention her natural beauty, why would she want to dance at the Gentlemen's Club?

"Fire," Georgia Mae spoke, remembering her reason for being there. "There's a gentleman here to see you. He's very affluent and generous with his money." She raised her eyebrow. "He wants to meet you."

"Affluent?" Monique frowned.

"Meaning he's very rich," Game said, taking a step closer. As she talked, Monique noticed a gold tooth inside her mouth. It looked kind of fly, even though she was sure it was fake. "He wants you to dance for him personally."

"I'm flattered," Monique said with genuine sincerity as she drew back in her chair, her hand over her heart, "but the show has been cancelled."

"No, he wants you to perform for him personally." Game walked over and sat on the edge of the dresser, partially blocking Monique's view of the mirror. She leaned forward and lowered her voice. "Fire, the man has more money than God." With her forehead wrinkled for emphasis she said, "He says he loves your show and that he's never been with a sista before."

"It figures," Monique laughed.

"The man is eighty years old. The last time I went to his place he wanted me to dress up in leather and beat the shit out of him."

"What?" Monique huffed, raising her eyebrows.

Game fidgeted as she continued, "He's what they call a masochist. It's a sexual per version where people get pleasure from being abused."

"No shit," Monique hissed, ill-tempered with Game for trying her like that.

"I . . . I . . . told him we would do a combo if he had the right amount of money." Game became a bundle of nerves as she ground the heel of her boot back and forth on the floor.

"Girl! I know the fuck you didn't!" Monique exclaimed, raising her voice.

Game removed her rear end off the dressing table as she rubbed her behind and stretched her neck from side to side. The fatigue from dancing wore heavily on her face. "I apologize, but since they cancelled your show I figured you could use the money."

"I can't believe you would do something like that without asking me!" Monique said hotly.

"The limousine should be here to pick us up in a few minutes. He usually pays three grand, but you can ask for five." Game slyly threw the gambit of money at Monique.

"Fi … five grand?" Monique stuttered as she sat straight up in her chair. Game had her attention now. She saw her reflection in the mirror … then Rasheed's. She blinked twice and saw dollar signs. "Five grand, huh?" Monique drawled slowly.

Game smiled with mischief as she walked up to the dresser and retrieved something from her purse, a packet of white powder. She poured a small mountain on the dresser tabletop and removed a crisp hundred-dollar bill from her purse. With long manicured fingernails she delicately rolled the bill into a tube.

"What's that?" Monique asked.

"Coke. Want a toot?"

"Nope." Monique looked at Game as she slid her chair back.

"When did you start using that?" Monique asked with feeling.

"Let's just put it like this," Game said, her eyes rolling to the back of her head after taking a snort of the powder. "I met a handsome black man that introduced me to a white girl with no legs. Her name was Cocaine. Since then, the brotha left, taking my money and stealing my heart. She's my new love. She loves me and says that she'll never leave me," Game mimicked in a singsong voice.

Monique instantly picked up on the gnawing hurt. Game was still suffering, trying to get over a broken heart. Drugs will never repair the ruins of love's demise. Monique started to tell her so, but it was not the right moment.

"You know you're gonna have to stop that," was all Monique said as she watched Game snort another line.

"Yeah, I'ma stop when you hook your girl up with one of them fine brothas." She leaned forward, snorted the last line and rose.

Monique could see the coke in her nose. Game was becoming a cocaine junkie and didn't even know it. Just then, there was a loud knock at the door causing both women to jump nervously as they exchanged looks. Quickly, Game placed the coke back in her purse. Monique walked to the door to open it. An elderly white man stood at the door. Monique instantly noticed something formidable about his features. He was dressed in all black, donning a matching hat and gloves. His clothes looked wet from the rain.

Game perked up. "Hey Johnson, you're early!"

Looking in her direction, the chauffeur slightly nodded his head. "Ma'am, if you ladies are ready, the car is waiting."

Game became excited as she looked in the mirror, wiped at her nose and checked her appearance. Satisfied, she buttoned up her jacket and briskly headed for the door as she gestured with a wave of her manicured hand. "Ta-ta love. You stayin' or you trying to get some of this free money?"

It took Monique less than a second to make up her mind. Five grand was a lot of money by any standards. "Damn girl, wait for meee!" Monique grabbed her purse and ran behind them.

Eleven

With umbrella in hand, the old chauffeur swayed slightly under the turbulent winds as he struggled to open the door. A strong gust of wind took his hat away, exposing his bald head. He looked down the street at his hat blowing in the wind as the wind further threatened to take him with it. Game's blond hair swirled around her face as she ducked to get inside the limousine.

Monique exhaled slowly before she got into the spacious car. Classical music popped from the speakers as they drove down the streets of New York in the early morning. Game crossed her long legs, one over the other, as she took out a miniature make-up case.

She pursed her thin lips as she looked into the mirror to apply her lipstick. "He lives in the Belleview Towers. It's a high rise that overlooks the city. Oprah and Bill Gates have suites there along with a few other celebrities."

"Who is this guy?" Monique asked.

"His name is Dr. Hugstible."

As Game talked, Monique leaned forward, craning her neck, eyes adjusting to the passing lights of the city and of cars passing by. Game's demeanor was tense, but still sophisticated.

"What I'm about to introduce you to is a world within a world. The filthy rich and the famous. In other words, the freaks and the shameless."

"You sure he don't want me to have sex with him or anything?" Monique asked nervously.

"I'm sure." Game laughed as she reached into her purse and retrieved her MAC pressed powder compact. She continued, "He just wants you to dominate him. He's into bondage—leather and whips and shit. The last time I was there I beat him while he wore pink panties and a bra."

"Get outta here!" Monique's mouth was wide open, forming an incredulous O. The car veered to the right, making a sharp turn.

Georgia Mae patted the sponge on her face, making sure her skin was flawless. "Why is he so interested in me?" Monique questioned as she looked out of the window watching the rain pour down.

Game snapped her compact closed with such force that it got Monique's attention. She ran her tongue over her teeth as if she was considering her words carefully. "The old man has been asking about you for quite some time, I just never told you. I told him that you weren't interested and figured as such. The truth is, in this business, when you find a gold mine, you don't tell everybody else. Hell, the old fart might die and leave me his entire estate," Game reasoned. "When they cancelled your show tonight, he went ballistic, saying he had to see you. It was real bizarre, like something straight out of the twilight zone, but then it dawned on me … something I learned my sophomore year of college."

"What's that?" Monique asked.

Game pulled in a deep breath and frowned with her tight lips forming a thin line across her face. "In college I was fortunate enough to have a black professor for my African American studies class. It started with twenty other white students in the class, including me. In two weeks I was the only white person there." Game made a face as she continued, "When you learn black history from a black perspective it's totally different than the watered down version that teaches Christopher Columbus discovered America and how civilization started with Rome. Anyway, girl …"

Baffled, Monique looked at Game wondering what the hell she was talking about.

Game continued, "During slavery it was a big thing for a white man to own female slaves, even poor whites, but the majority of rich white men had a harem of female slaves just for their own personal satisfaction. Even back then, the white man had sexual lust for black women. They maintained their powerful positions because of all of the money they made off of slavery. The profit was something like 1500%. A white male with a black female mistress was an acceptable part of Southern life, even a rite of manhood. A young white man wasn't a man until he had sex with a black woman. Unfortunately, the majority of the black women were raped. Some of the stronger black women openly chose suicide rather than continuing to be raped, molested and degraded. We were told that one black woman even cut her master's head off."

"And?" Monique said. She was clearly disturbed by what Game was saying, but wondered what all of this had to do with her.

"Well …" Game shrugged her shoulders uncomfortably. "I feel like an outsider lookin' in. Dr. Hugstible is the grandchild of a rich former slave owner. It just seems like white men have this secret fetish for black women that dates back so far, but they try to hide it."

"Girl, please. They don't try to hide that shit. It's taboo and they love it. Just like white women who openly have a thing for black men." She looked at Georgia Mae with a raised eyebrow.

Game had to giggle because she did prefer a black man over a white one any day. She swatted Monique's arm, hitting her as the two women laughed like old friends. Then with a serious expression, Game added, "I ain't no white woman, at least I swear to God I don't feel like one. I'm a black woman trapped in a white woman's body."

Monique corrected her by playfully saying, "Naw girl, you mean a black woman trapped in a white woman's skin, 'cause you damn sho'll got a black girl's junk in your trunk." They laughed.

Monique fixed herself a strong drink from the bar and for the first time in her life, she listened to, and enjoyed, classical music as she watched Game remove a Philly blunt from her purse and expertly bust it open with her fingernail. They rode the rest of the way in silence as they blazed the blunt in the back seat of the limo. The dark rainy night welcomed them to a destination of the freaks and the shameless.

Dr. Hugstible greeted them amicably at the door. He pecked Game on her cheek as they entered the penthouse suite. Monique was in awe of its grandiose splendor. She was also taken by surprise at the stature of the doctor. He had wide thin shoulders, bony hands, and narrow hips. He stood a little over six feet tall with lank gray hair and a large fleshy nose with spider veins in it, but there was something about his eyes – the glint of a sparkle.

In his day, the doctor used to be a ladies' man. Now his body was riddled with age. His old, wrinkled skin barely hung on his bones. His shifty eyes and thick gray eyebrows twitched as he spoke to Game. Monique stood stoic with a generic polite smile plastered on her face as she tried to mask her discomfort. She slid her eyes off the doctor over to Game.

"Fire, I'm honored to meet you," the doctor said, catching her off-guard. He extended his hand out to her. Hesitantly, she shook it. His hand felt moist and clammy as he smiled with teeth fit for a horse, too big for his narrow mouth and shrunken head.

An older Mexican woman, the maid, entered the room. She was dressed in a white A-line skirt with a black apron. They followed the doctor into the main parlor. The walls were adorned with expensive antique oil paintings. Next to a large picture window sat a white grand piano. In the corner to her left was a seven-foot-tall knight in shining armor. For some reason, the huge statue spooked Monique. It reminded her of the horror movies she used to watch when she was a little girl. Outside the window, the thunder clapped and lightning lit up the night sky. Monique flinched.

"I've always enjoyed the aesthetics of beautiful women, especially black women, but you, my dear, are beyond beautiful. You're like an exquisite African rose in the summertime," the doctor said as his eyes undressed her.

Was that a white man's version of putting his mack down? Monique thought as she watched the doctor crinkle his nose at her while he scratched his privates and continued to let his hand linger there, touching himself. Game looked on, annoyed, as she strutted to the other side of the room and placed her purse on the floor and began to undress. Somewhere in the distance a clock loudly chimed.

"Honey, you never did say a price for both of us," Game said, in an attempt to jock for position over Monique. It was as if Monique had some kind of spell on the doctor.

Game arched her back, thrusting out her supple breasts. The doctor continued to ignore her while staring at Monique like a hungry wolf. He lickedhis lips and rubbed his hands together anxiously.

"Fire, what do you feel is appropriate?" he asked with a strained smile on his lips. His teeth were so large they overlapped in his mouth. He walked up closer to Monique as she stood aloof, even though she felt his nearness like a second skin. Every nerve and fiber in her body was alive, alert, tingling. She knew that she was totally out of her element. From across the room, Game looked on with contempt.

"Sugar, we have every intention of serving every one of your needs and desires, as only you want us to serve you, but I'd rather you make an offer and I'll let you know if the price is right," Monique said in the sweetest voice she could while doing her best impression of a strip tease as she slowly undressed.

As the doctor watched, a trickle of saliva dribbled from the corner of his mouth. Monique eyed Game, searching for her approval. Game slyly winked her eye, but her face was smug. She was sending Monique mixed signals. The doctor reached out and touched Monique on the shoulder. His bony fingers were cold as his hand trembled. He rubbed at her skin almost as if to see if the color would rub off. The doctor was fascinated with Monique. As she removed his hand, Monique realized that she had been holding her breath.

"I'll pay you seven thousand dollars."

At the sound of the money Monique kicked her shoe off with so much force that it sailed across the room, landing next to the knight. Game shot Monique a warning stare as she walked toward the doctor with her arms folded over her breasts.

"Surely, you can't be talking about seven thousand measly dollars for us to split?"

The doctor turned, giving her a look as if she were an intruder. "No, I was thinking more to the tune of five thousand for Fire and two for you."

Taken aback, Game threw her head back like she had been slapped in the face. "That's bullshit!" she screeched, shooting daggers at the old man with jagged green eyes.

Instantly Monique caught on to what was happening and decided to play her hand with a straight poker face. Taking a step forward she boldly announced, "We came here together and we leave here together. Either you accept our price and pay the same for both of us or we walk," Monique said adamantly with her hands on her hips.

The old man bunched his lips to talk as a muffled groan escaped from somewhere deep in his throat like a man lost for words. Game couldn't help but smirk with joy as she struggled to suppress a smile. The old man took a step back and placed one hand in his pocket and the other underneath his chin, as if contemplating his next thought. Slowly, Game started to get dressed as she watched the drama unfold. Now she felt like an outsider.

The moment lingered. Monique realized she had played her hand and lost. She padded across the carpet to retrieve her shoe.

The old man, disgruntled, responded, "Okay … okay, as you wish. Five thousand a piece."

Monique stopped in her tracks, looking at the spooky statue as she reached for her shoe. She thought about a man being behind the steel cage of the mask. She turned around and smiled so broadly it hurt her cheeks. Amused, the doctor couldn't help but laugh. Monique Cheeks had played the game well, so far.

Game just looked on, confused, as once again she wondered about the forbidden taboo, the white man's lascivious lust for black flesh. Game was familiar with the boudoir inside the doctor's suite. It was about the size of a small chic clothing store. An assortment of brand new clothes and costumes lined the walls. Monique did a full turn in the middle of the floor, mouth agape. There were even a few designer clothes with the tags still on them – Gucci, Louis Vuitton. She saw some Rocawear and Dolce and Gabbana also. Instantly she regretted not bringing her big purse. She was sure the old man wouldn't miss any of the stuff if it came up missing.

"You go girl!" Game exclaimed joyfully as she gave Monique a high-five. "Five thousand a piece. Wow! You damn sure got guts."

"You said he was willing to pay five grand."

"I lied. I was just trying to persuade you to come," Game said, still excited about the money. Monique just shook her head at Game as she continued to look at all the beautiful clothes and exotic costumes.

They quickly got dressed. Monique had on a black, leather, crotchless catwoman outfit. She refused to put on the mask. As it was, Game was cracking up laughing at her. Game wore a skin-tight red devil outfit. The pants were too small for her big butt, so she had to wear her thong instead. Game continued to chuckle as they exited the room and headed down the hall.

"Bitch, what's so damn funny?" Monique asked, amused by Game's humor. They were both still high from the blunt they had smoked earlier.

Game was curled over in laughter as she held her side. "You …you … look like a cat burglar dressed up in … that get-up," Game managed to say as she roared with hysterical laughter, grabbing at her sides like she couldn't breathe.

"At least I found clothes I could fit into and my ass ain't too big to get into my costume."

"Aw, bitch, stop hatin'," Game said with a giggle as she fought for control of her laughter. "Once we walk through that door …"

Game looked down at Monique's clothes and giggled. Monique rolled her eyes as she promised herself that this would be her last time ever smoking with this chick. Game tried to speak again as her eyes sparkled with giddy laughter. "Once we step through that door it's showtime."

Monique swallowed the lump in her throat. Unlike Game, she still had the jitters and regardless of how much she tried to relax, the creepy old white man still disturbed her.

"The last time I was here he wanted me to beat him. It was really disgusting." Game made a face at the memory as a wisp of blond hair fell over her eyes.

"I don't know about you, but for five grand, girl, please, I'm about ta beat all the pink off his peanut-head ass."

Game burst out laughing, placing her hand over her mouth.

"I swear, I'll never smoke with you again," Monique huffed as they slowly walked. Up ahead, at the end of the hall, the doctor appeared. He had changed into a simple black robe with gray loafers. Monique stutter-stepped when she saw him.

Game giggled at her antics as she nudged Monique. "Look!"

The doctor stood with his hands inside his pockets, his eyes glued to Monique as both women approached. His left eye twitched as if he was in some type of pain. Game sobered up fast as she wiped at the tuft of hair in front of her forehead with the back of her hand. "Here comes the perverted part. Watch this."

"Huh?" Monique said as she watched the doctor bow his head and disrobe. Underneath he wore a pink garter belt with matching bra, sheer panties and black stockings. Game barbed a giggle that threatened to erupt into a boisterous cackle.

"Goddamnitmuthafuckingsonofabitch! Look at him!" Monique intoned as her jaw dropped, aghast by the sight of the old man.

The doctor's body was covered with long, prickly gray hairs. His skinny ribs were visible and he had dense patches of hair on his chest and private area. He looked like a starved bear with a bad case of mange. A bush of furry hair protruded from between his scrawny legs. His withered penis was about the size of an infant's.

"Oh, mother of punishment, I have been a bad boy, please don't hurt me," the doctor mimicked in a child's voice.

Monique made a face as she exchanged glances with Game. The doctor fell on his hands and knees groveling in mock penitent tones. Monique could see his skinny backbone through all the hair and his sickly pale skin. Game strutted over to him with all the confidence of a woman who was used to playing the sick game of sadomasochism. On the floor, the doctor had an assortment of toys that he liked to be punished with – a whip, something that resembled a water hose and even a thin chain that looked like it was made of gold. Game picked up the flexible hose and began to lightly swat the doctor on his fanny as she smirked at Monique who was barely able to contain her laughter. Acting, the old man shuddered and whimpered at her feet as Monique looked on in disbelief.

"Bad boy … bad boy," Game said with animation as she played the charade.

The doctor looked up at her. "Harder! Harder!"

Tightly, Monique closed her eyes and then opened them. She was overcome with grief and despair. This old white man had all this wealth. Just looking around at all the opulent splendor, it disturbed her in a way that she could not explain. She thought about what Game had said on the ride over. A world of the filthy rich and famous … the freaks and the shameless.

Once again Monique looked at Game frolicking with the doctor as she lightly tapped him on his rear. He didn't appear to be enjoying the game. Monique couldn't help but think to herself, white folks are crazy

She felt something deep within her stir, a combination of envy, jealousy and even rage. All her life her family had been struggling just to survive. She thought about the neighbor next door, the fifteen-year-old girl who had a baby and dumped it in the dumpster and all the single mothers she knew who were struggling. She thought about herself and what she was doing, all because of shattered dreams. At twenty-one she should have been about to graduate from college, but no. A world of hatred began to swell inside of her, in that sacred place that she had tried to shelter from the cold and bitter world—that place in her heart.

To her utter dismay, she watched as the doctor groveled toward her, crawling on all fours like a dog. Disgusting! He was at her feet. Game made a swinging motion with her hand, indicating to Monique to hit the doctor. Paralyzed with fear Monique just stood there, frozen. The moment lingered like a clock whose hands had stalled.

"Mother, don't hurt me," the doctor said.

"Pst, hit him, hit him!" Game persuaded with a concerned look on her face.

"Punish me," the doctor clamored and looked up at Monique sideways.

In the corner of her eye she saw Game gesturing with her hand for her to strike the doctor. Monique realized she couldn't do it as she looked down at the pale ghastly skin of the doctor with his butt tooted up in the air. God, she wished this grotesque scene would go away.

"Pst, Monique, damnit girl, do it!" Game hissed with her voice on edge.

"Punish me." The doctor's voice sounded like a plea.

Two voices both urged her on in a world within a world, the freaks and the shameless.

I can't do this, Monique said to herself. She looked at Game with an apologetic face. Just then, she felt something wet and clammy on her foot. She looked down to see the doctor licking her feet. Something inside her snapped as red flashed behind her eyes. Images of a baby in a dumpster flashed before her eyes, just as she had seen it on the news. She picked up the thick whip a few feet away from her and totally lost control.

She watched herself go crazy as she brought the whip down hard on the doctor's back. It made a deadly whistling sound in the air as it connected with flesh. The doctor opened his mouth to scream, but no words came out, only a pained expression of pure agony. Finally, from somewhere in the pit of his gut, a simmering guttural sound segued into a protracted howl that ended in a haunting scream. Frantically, he began to rub the area where she had just struck him as if it were on fire. Monique brought the whip down again, this time with more force, causing the doctor to howl.

She struck him, again and again. Violently she swung the whip causing it to whistle in the air. Her face was a mask of fury, lips pulled back with malice scrawled across it, intent on inflicting as much pain as possible. With each blow, she felt like she was releasing pent-up emotions as she escaped into of a part of her mind that she did not know existed—she crossed the thin line between sanity and insanity. She never knew that inflicting so much pain could feel so good. Too good. Tears began to fill her eyes. Once again she thought about the baby in the dumpster, this life and the brutal ways of the world for a single woman trying to raise a child.

Whip!

Whip! Whip!

The doctor began to wither and retreat as he put up a weary hand to ward off the blows. His body was grossly covered with red marks with a few of the marks now bleeding.

"Stop it! Stop it!" Game yelled loudly as she placed one of her hands over her mouth in shock.

In a trance-like state, Monique continued to beat him in a fit of rage, drawing blood from the doctor's back and lower extremities. He desperately attempted to get away from her. She was a raving maniac and was giving him more than his five thousand dollars' worth. She was trying to kill him.

The doctor crawled under a table. Monique wasted no time grabbing one of his scrawny legs and yanking him so hard across the floor that she gave him rug burns. She began to violently punch and kick him in the face and in the head and arms, whirling in a blur of motion.

The doctor stopped resisting and lay there motionless as she continued to pummel him. Game rushed over just as Monique was about to swing again. She caught her fist in mid-air, spun Monique around and placed her in a bear hug. They tripped and fell down with Game on top. Monique was panting loudly and her body was covered in sweat.

"Monique, you're going to kill him, for Godsake!" Game said as she looked down at her. She could feel her heaving. It was the only sound that echoed in the stillness of the parlor.

Dr. Hugstible lay motionless at the other end of the floor as blood trickled from both his nose and his mouth. One of his large horse-sized teeth lay in the middle of the floor as a silent reminder of the tragedy that had just taken place.

"Oh my God! Listen," Game's voice quivered. She could feel Monique's heart beating against her chest.

"Listen to what?" Monique asked, still winded.

For some strange reason she looked up at the artwork on the cathedral ceiling—a nude boy with angelic wings, aiming a bow and arrow.

"It's too quiet." They both sat up, eyes alert, ears astute, listening to the unnerving silence. They helped each other up and tiptoed over to the doctor.

"He's dead! You killed him," Game said. Her face was a ball of anguish. "Feel his heart," she whispered.

"Uh-uh, I'm not touching him," Monique replied, taking a step back.

They were both startled by a noise. It sounded like someone clearing their throat to get their attention. Standing ominously in the shadows at the end of the hall were the chauffeur and the maid. Their gloomy figures frightened them.

"Oh, shit, look!" Game uttered. "Please go feel for his heartbeat. We need to see if he's still alive. Maybe we can get him to a hospital."

Slowly, Monique walked over toward the doctor. She could feel her heart racing so fast in her chest that it felt like she was going to faint. She bent down and reached out to feel his neck for a pulse. Her eyes darted all over the place like she expected someone to grab her. Gently, with two fingers, she touched the doctor's neck as a million ideas ran wild through her head. The two figures stood at the end of the hall watching. How was she going to make an escape? Was it possible for a black woman in a crotchless catwoman suit to catch a cab in the wee hours of the morning in Belleview Heights?

Rasheed's face appeared on the screen of her panicked mind. Her hand trembled as she searched the doctor's neck for a pulse.

The chauffeur started to walk toward them briskly. He had something in his hand. A gun? A phone?

"Aw, shit," Game muttered fearfully.

Monique couldn't feel any pulse. The doctor was dead. Monique looked up just as the chauffeur entered the room. As if on cue, the doctor reached up and grabbed Monique's hand.

"Boo!"

Monique leapt up so fast that she stumbled and fell on her butt.

The doctor roared with laughter at the antics of the black girl. His tooth was missing, one of his eyes was partially swollen closed, black and blue bruises covered his body and his gray hair stood up like he had stuck his finger in a light socket. He began laughing like a man that truly got a kick out of playing a prank on someone. After he caught his breath, still giddy, he said, "My dear lady, that was mar-ve-lous. I got 'cha, huh?" He laughed some more as he cupped his jaw with his hand, twisting it from side to side to see how badly it was broken. He winced noticeably.

"She almost killed you!" Game stepped up and screamed at the old man. She was infuriated. A thick blue vein protruded from her forehead as her jagged green eyes flashed optic slants of anger.

"On the contrary, my dear, she merely facilitated me in a game I immensely enjoy playing. Frankly, you need to take lessons from her."

"Whaaat!?" Game screeched.

As Monique looked on, a wave of relief washed over her. Thank God the old man was alive. As Game continued to curse out the doctor, Monique's heart rate began to steady. She opened and closed her fist, examining her knuckles as all she could think about was getting her money and getting the hell out of there.

They rode in the back of the limo in total silence as the rain pelted the car windows. The car stopped at a red light across the street from a liquor store. Vaguely, an orange neon light flashed inside the car, illuminating Game's face. Monique tried her best to ignore her ill disposition since they had left the doctor's residence.

"That cracka blew my high," Game said hotly, causing Monique to glance sideways at her.

Sometimes Game talked just like a black person and it continued to amaze Monique. The car pulled away from the light causing them to lean back in their seats. Monique shuffled through the new, crisp hundred-dollar bills in her hand. Five thousand dollars, just as the good doctor promised.

"I'm never going back there again," Game said as she reached into her purse for a Philly blunt that she quickly began to break open. "What about you?"

Monique's mind was someplace else.

Game leered at her as she twisted the blunt. "I said I'm never going back there. What about you?" she asked a little louder this time.

Silence. Speeding, the car veered as it changed lanes. Monique looked up from the money. "I almost killed him," she said out loud. Her comment was totally out of place.

Somehow Game seemed not to notice as she replied, "Sometimes my own people, white people, embarrass the hell out of me." Game lit the blunt with a gold cigarette lighter and inhaled deeply on the potent weed.

"Umph, you can say that again … about your own people embarrassing you," Monique said, her voice distant.

"What happened back there anyway?" Game took a pull off the blunt. "At first you were scared to death to hit him and then you just went the fuck off."

"I dunno." Monique shrugged her shoulders. "At first I was scared, then something about him provoked me. I think it was when he was licking my feet. Not only was I disgusted, I felt violated. Once I hit him with that whip it felt like I was releasing all my hurt and anger … about the baby in the dumpster."

"Huh?"

"Yeah, I almost killed him. What you said about this being a world within a world. Well, I've never had this much money given to me at one time in my entire life," Monique said, holding up the money.

Game arched her brow at her and took another pull off the blunt. Monique continued, "In fact, in my world, crackheads would beat the brakes off that white man for much less than five grand. They would do it for five dollars, on an installment plan."

Game chuckled and gagged on the blunt as the aroma filled the car. She attempted to pass it to Monique, but she declined.

Game tossed her blond hair back as headlights passed, lighting up her face. "You had that same wild look in your eyes that night you fought Tatyana in the dressing room."

"What look?" Monique questioned with a raised brow.

"The look of a person possessed by demons."

"Yeah, well, it may have looked like I was, but the little move you did by grabbing my wrists and placing me in whatever kind of hold that was …" Monique remembered how Game had held her.

"I have a black belt in karate. Sorry, I wasn't trying to hurt you. I told you my mom had me entering all kinds of talent shows. She had me practicing martial arts at seven years old."

Monique thought back to Game's awesome stage performance. Her walking on her hands and grabbing the pole with her butt.

"You would have killed that old man if I hadn't stopped you," Game said, mentally pinning Monique against a brick wall of reality.

She leaned forward and poured herself a drink from the bar as Monique let the window down. The cool night air whooshed around the car with its tiny raindrops. Monique licked the rim of her top lip, savoring the taste. She closed her eyes and saw Rasheed's face … again.

How can I make him understand? she thought as Game spoke.

"I told you I was a black woman trapped in a white woman's body, and now I've introduced you to the white world. Now it's time for you to introduce me to the other world, the black world."

As Game spoke, it dawned on Monique that she was dead serious. She was actually trying to replace a broken heart with a broken heart. That was what was going to happen if Game got what she wanted—a brotha. At least that was Monique's opinion.

"Girl, trust me when I say that these men today ain't shit. They just wanna hit it and move on to the next piece of ass. Stay on your side of the tracks. They'll run through you like water."

Game was instantly offended. "What? I know what I want," Game shot back.

"Are you willing to deal with the changes, their instability?" Monique questioned as she thought about Rasheed.

"I had your back in more ways than one, Monique." Game waved her envelope filled with money in the air.

Monique then looked down at her envelope. She was right, if it weren't for Game, she wouldn't have five thousand dollars in her hand.

"Well, I guess I do owe you that much." Monique had to admit, Game not only talked black, she also dressed and behaved just like a black woman, so it shouldn't be any problem. "You know you my girl. I'ma see if I can hook you up."

Game smiled in acknowledgement as they rode the rest of the way in silence.

Twelve

Rasheed Smith

A bright moon held Rasheed's spirit captive as he stared up at the sky. A lone star in the galaxy sparkled. In the distance a cat screamed and a door slammed. Across the street, an old Marvin Gaye tune blared from one of the neighbor's houses, "What's Goin'On?"

As Rasheed stared up at the celestial heavens, a full moon stared back at him with a sly grin. It was 4:47 a.m. He sat on his grandma's front porch. The old decrepit house was the only home he had ever known. The house was so old that when anyone stepped on the porch, a slight noise would be heard inside the house, a poor man's burglar alarm, always causing Grandma Hattie to wake from a sound sleep.

Rasheed fanned mosquitoes absent-mindedly as he was lost in his thoughts, thoughts that barged their way into his twenty-two-year-old mind. Monique dancing nude, parading her body for other men to see. All for the love of money. "Damn!"

He thought about his future. What if he didn't get drafted into the pros? His prospects didn't look too bright then. He was a convicted felon. He worried about his son, his needs, life's basic necessities, school clothes and education.

"Shit!" Rasheed cursed as he raked his fingers through his curly hair.

He looked up to see a dope fiend walking down the sidewalk doing a reconnaissance mission through the neighborhood, looking for something to steal. Rasheed recognized the man as Tyson Harmon. He lived a few blocks away. He and Rasheed played ball against each other. Tyson was a better athlete than Rasheed at one time. That was until he started hanging with the wrong crew.

Just then, in the opposite direction, Rasheed looked up to see headlights approaching. It was Monique's car, a late model Honda. The brakes squeaked as she pulled into the yard. One of her headlights was dim. Rasheed sat in the darkness as he watched her, a girl he had loved since she was fourteen years old. As she got out of the car, he watched her bounce up the walkway on the ball of her toes. Monique Cheeks was born to be a dancer. She even walked like a dancer. He fought to contain his breathing as he realized he didn't know what to say or even where to start.

"Mo," he whispered, softly saying her name, careful not to startle her as he stood.

She stutter-stepped, surprised. "Baby, what you doing out here?"

For some reason her words seemed to stir his emotions as the incandescent moon's glow shimmered off her shiny black hair and delicate features, causing her silhouette to appear like an enigma in his mind. He needed to see her face up close, touch her, and feel her, his woman.

"I couldn't sleep … had a lot on my mind," he said, answering her question.

Instantly, she recognized that his voice was filled with hurt. Her heart sunk in her chest as she watched him sit back down. She walked up to him and stood between his legs, embracing his head in her arms, pressing his face against her bosom as she rocked him.

"I saw Jack Lemon today," was all Rasheed could think to say.

Monique pulled away from him. "He's out?"

"Yeah, and crazy as hell this time."

"He's always been a little off if you ask me."

"Naw, but it's worse this time."

"I don't know how it can be that much worse. Even though he's our friend and we've known him since high school, Jack has killed a lot of people. How did he get out this time?"

"He won an appeal. He gave me some money to give to you, too." Rasheed cleared his throat. "Dude on some serious death before dishonor shit."

"What about Gina?"

"I dunno, but he's acting like he's god of the universe. He told me she got him out of prison. Tomorrow he's going to stop by here—"

"I'm sorr y for what I said," Monique blurted out, changing the subject, taking both of them to that place that neither wanted to go—the present moment.

"My son has a father and I have a man. I love you so much," she whispered in the dark as her words stuck in her throat. She blinked back tears as she spoke.

Reaching in her purse, she removed a wad of cash, placing the bills in his hand.

"What's this?" he asked.

She took a step back and looked at him. "It's five thousand dollars." She couldn't muster the courage to tell him how she earned the money and he knew better than to ask.

"I'll stop dancing and go back to the bakery, but I'm beggin' you please just let me work two more weeks and then I'll stop," Monique pleaded as she gently held his handsome face in her hands.

"Baby, it's up to you if you want to let me do the magazine shoot. Chances are they won't accept me anyway, but if they do, I'll have enough money to go back to college and maybe buy a house, or at least put a down payment on one."

"Two weeks, huh?" Rasheed muttered, tossing the idea around in his head.

"Uh-huh … ouch!" she screeched, slapping her arm. "Damn mosquitoes."

He chuckled as he palmed her butt. "Two weeks and you promise you'll quit?"

"Yes, yes." Monique beamed with joy and pulled him close to her. "Baby, I promise I'll quit. I know how bad this whole thing hurts you. You've always liked to watch me dance. I never wanted you to lose respect for me." She looked into his eyes and the starry night suddenly took on a whole new meaning. "Rasheed, can I make love to you?" The timbre of her voice was soft as the night breeze, mellow like a song.

She grinded her torso against him, closing her eyes, envisioning him deep inside of her. Up the street a police car cruised as its searchlights rudely disturbed the night, illuminating the streets like a miniature sun, bouncing, roaming from place to place, in search of something.

Finally, the light settled on Rasheed and Monique, causing her to flinch and turn around to see what was going on.

Rasheed stood up, shielding his eyes from the intrusive light with his hands.

Suddenly two officers got out of their cars with their guns drawn.

"You, the black male, slowly come off the porch with your hands in the air where we can see them," an authoritative, deep baritone voice commanded.

Rasheed could tell it was a white officer. The lights blinded him as he squinted his eyes at the bright lights and went for his wallet.

"Officer, there's a mistake. I live—"

"Freeze!" a voice ordered on the fringe of panic.

Rasheed heard the distinctive sound of guns being cocked. The deadly sound resonated in the still of the night.

"Please, no. We live here!" Monique shrieked. She knew all too well about the excessive force of the NYPD.

"This is bullshit!" Rasheed mumbled under his breath.

"What's going on out there?" Grandma Hattie asked from inside the door. "Ra, baby, you alright?"

"Yeah, Ma, I'm alright. Go back inside," Rasheed was able to say without letting on to his fear.

"No, he ain't alright! These damn fools out here got guns pulled on us," Monique belted out, gesturing with her hands as she stomped her foot in frustration.

Tentatively Rasheed walked down the steps with his hands high in the air. The officer rushed him in an attempt to slam him to the ground.

"Hold up, hold up, man!" Rasheed said, resisting being slammed to the ground.

"Stop it! Stop it!" Monique wailed.

"You women go back inside and let us handle this situation," the officer commanded.

"My boy ain't done nuttin' ta nobody. Y'all leave him be!" Grandma Hattie said, walking onto the porch as she clasped her old threadbare robe around her.

When Rasheed saw his grandma walk onto the porch he stopped resisting and let the officer slam him to ground.

Monique screamed, "Rasheed!" He hit the hard pavement in a thud, unsettling dirt and dust in the artificial smoggy haze.

The officer jumped on Rasheed's back, kneeing him in the spine, shoving his face in the dirt. Rasheed grunted in pain as the officer struck him in the head with his fist and placed the gun to his temple.

The officer whispered in a gravelly voice, "Nigger, you move again and I'll blow your goddamn brains out right here in front of your granny and that loud-mouth bitch. You didn't know who you was fuckin' wit', huh?" The officer attempted to show his partner just how to control one of them "wanna be bad niggers".

This was not Rasheed's first encounter with the boys in blue, the power hungry demons who were supposed to serve and protect him. What made this painstakingly humiliating for Rasheed was that it was a black officer who held a gun to his head threatening to kill him in front of his family. He was obviously trying to impress his white buddy. Rasheed hated for his grandmother and Monique to see him like this. A sour taste shocked his taste buds as blood co-mingled with dirt covered his palate.

"What do we have here?" the officer said as he snatched a wad of cash out of Rasheed's pocket.

"Hey, that's my girl's money!" Rasheed yelled.

"Yeah, and I'm motherfuckin' Santa Claus," the officer retorted derisively, kneeing Rasheed in the back.

Monique couldn't take any more of the madness. She attempted to run down the steps, but Grandma Hattie grabbed her arm with surprising strength and shot her a warning glance that told her to let her take over.

At eighty-eight, she had seen more than her share of brutality and abuse of her people. There was a period in time when there was such a thing as "strange fruit hanging from trees". That was during a time when young black men and women were lynched and hung from trees, merely because of the color of their skin, for some festive occasion. Some say that is where the word "picnic" was coined, from "pick-a-nigger."

Grandma Hattie ambled to the front of the porch. A few neighbors trickled out of their houses onto their front porches after being awakened by the commotion. An elderly black woman in slippers and a housecoat who had a large German Shepherd at her side watched her neighbor of over forty years talk to the police.

Grandma Hattie said vehemently, "That's my grand boy, he ain't done nuttin' ta nobody. His name is Rasheed Smith. He plays basketball for St. John's." She had focused all of her attention on the white cop because she knew a black man trying to impress whites was the most dangerous person on the face of the planet.

"Sir, my boy is a good boy," she spoke in a small voice as she cast her eyes down at the ground, a submissive posture to go with her poignant plea. The white cop went for it.

As he searched his memory bank for the recollection of the name, he spoke, "Oh, I know 'em. He's the kid who scored sixty-one points a few weeks back. They had him on SportsCenter."

"Yes sir, that's my boy," Grandma Hattie said, slightly nodding her head.

People began to gather around, gawking. A van and an SUV pulled up with young adults who had just left a party.

The white officer frowned at his partner. "Ma'am, we had a call for a prowler in the area." He then walked over to his partner.

"Tate, that ain't him. Let him up."

The youngsters got out of their cars and walked over to the melee. "Hey, that's Rasheed Smith on the ground." The officer was still on top of Rasheed, whispering threats into his ear when the bottle came whistling by, barely missing the black cop's head.

The cop leapt off Rasheed, eyes ablaze with fury as he searched the crowd for the culprit who had thrown the bottle.

An angry voice vociferously yelled, "Y'all leave that man alone!"

Rasheed got off the ground slowly. To his horror, he saw his Lil' Malcolm standing in the doorway beside the dog with a terrified expression on his face. Something panged in Rasheed's chest. God, why did his son have to see him like this? This evil tradition, police brutality in the ghetto, was handed down from one generation to the next. Two other police cruisers drove up as more people started to gather around.

Lieutenant Anthony Brown got out of his car to the raucous sound of hecklers, a sign that trouble was brewing. As he weaved through the crowd of onlookers, he politely urged the people to go back to their houses. He was taken aback by the sight of Grandma Hattie. Then his attention focused on the kid, Rasheed, all covered in dirt with blood coming from his mouth.

"Hi Grandma Hattie, what's going on here?" he asked the woman who had single-handedly raised an entire neighborhood with love and affection.

She hobbled down the stairs. "This Sambo nigger here is harassing my boy!" she said, pointing a scrawny finger at the black officer.

"The boy tried to resist when I told him to raise his hands."

"You tellin' a damn lie," Monique interjected as she walked down the stairs.

"I took this money off of him." The black officer showcased a satisfied grin on his face as he talked to his young superior.

"That's my damn money. I worked for it!" Monique screeched.

"If you don't have a receipt for it, I'ma have to take it."

"Can he do that?" Monique turned toward the Lieutenant.

Her eyebrows knotted together. Her voice had given way to a hint of fear.

The young Lieutenant shrugged his shoulders nodding his head, indicating "yes."

"I guess he also can walk up here on private property and beat the hell out of an innocent man, too, huh?" she said indignantly as she boldly got in the black officer's face.

The Lieutenant raised his brow with the word "beat." Monique had his attention.

"He just came on my property and threw Rasheed to the ground and placed a gun to his head," Grandma Hattie said.

"That's a lie," the black officer barked. The commotion heated up as vulgar words were exchanged back and forth. For some reason, Rasheed just stood there impassive with his brown eyes transfixed on his son, the child who was destined to inherit a torn legacy of broken promises and shattered dreams, handed down from father to son, from generation to generation.

Rasheed felt numb and dehumanized as rage and humiliation consumed him. He was powerless to act on this most profane violation, denied a man's right to defend himself and his family. Rasheed felt that if he couldn't kill the officer for the egregious violation of dishonoring him in front of his family, then what was the use of giving the officer the satisfaction of knowing that he was humiliated to the point of being tormented with anger – a conscious man's logic in dealing with defeat.

As Monique and the officer argued, Grandma Hattie sneaked alongside the black officer and with surprising quickness, snatched the money out of his hand. The crowd roared with laughter as the old woman placed the money in her brassiere. The black cop moved toward Grandma Hattie like he was going to take the money back.

Rasheed stepped in between them, bumping his chest against the black cop. "I'll die for that old woman right there. Now you put your hands on her, try me, you sell-out-ass nigga," Rasheed threatened, his nostrils flared, eyes bulging with disdain. The right side of his face was covered with dirt.

"Back off, Tate, and you, Rasheed, take your butt back into the house," Lieutenant Brown said sternly.

"But what about the money?" the cop asked with a frown on his face.

"What about we press charges on your sorry ass?" Monique huffed.

The white cop walked up. It was obvious by his flushed red cheeks that he didn't want anything to do with the abuse of the kid.

"I'm sorry about what happened—"

"Sorr y about what?" Monique cut him off. "The NYPD give a black man a beatdown on the regular, twenty-four seven, like fuckin' recreation. Now you got brain-dead-ass niggas doin' all the dirty work. The worst thing that white folks could have done was give a black man a little authority because he becomes worse than them." Monique cringed when she realized she had cursed in front of Ms. Hattie. "Oops," she said, covering her mouth.

"I could not have said it better, child," Grandma Hattie admitted.

The white cop looked at Lieutenant Brown. "Sir, there may have been some excessive force on the part of Tate. You know how he gets at times." He looked at his partner who angrily stalked away.

Lieutenant Brown turned to Rasheed with a raised brow as if to ask a question. Rasheed stood on the porch, now holding his son. The expression on his face was that of a man determined to hide his wounded pride.

"You want to file charges or should I report him to Internal Affairs?"

"No! You don't file charges on a man that steps on your land and disrespects you and your family by physically abusing you in front of your woman and kid." Rasheed raised his voice, one of his eyes red as if he had fought to control his emotions. "You file 'vengeance to kill by any means necessary' whenever he crosses your path again." Rasheed's jaw was clenched tight. "And you," Rasheed addressed Officer Tate, "Grandma Hattie raised you. You grew up right down the street from here. You used to call yourself a Black Panther back in the day and now this is what you bring back to your very own community? You a mad-dog-ass nigga."

Rasheed had a pained expression on his face as his voice cracked.

"I took this job to help y'all from getting hurt," Lieutenant Brown reminded Rasheed. "You can't hold one bad cop's actions against all the good cops who are trying to help the community."

Monique and Grandma Hattie just watched the exchange of words. The crowd started to leave as a murmur of shallow voices announced their departure. A patrol car pulled up in front of the yard. Rasheed recognized Tyson Harmon in the back seat, the junkie who had passed the house earlier.

A white officer called from the patrol car window, "Lieutenant, we found the prowler. The suspect was trying to break into a car a few blocks from here."

It dawned on Rasheed that Tyson was the cause of all this mess. The ironic part was, Tyson Harmon was Lieutenant Brown's nephew. Rasheed watched Brown peer into the car and then kicked the dirt in disgust.

"Shit!" he muttered under his breath and turned to Grandma Hattie. "I'll stop by for dinner after church." He didn't give her a chance to answer as he turned and walked briskly toward the patrol car with Tyson in the back seat.

The crowd had already dispersed. For the first time, the old dog tried to bark—a sound that could have passed for a human cough.

They walked inside the old house. As expected, Grandma Hattie preached about right and wrong. She said she knew that something bad was about to happen because all night her right leg had been bothering her and the last time that happened was when they tried to evict her out of her house due to a tax error. Finally, she yawned and gave Rasheed his money back and shuffled back to her room, humming an old church hymn. The baby had fallen asleep in his father's arms.

Monique spied the soul of a battered man as Rasheed limped away to put their son back to bed. She could sense his pain as only a black woman could. They hadn't spoken since Rasheed placed the baby at the foot of his bed and disrobed in the semi-darkness of the room, the same room she had lost her virginity in when she was seventeen.

With his shoulders slumped, she watched him trudge to the bathroom to take a shower. She hated to see him hurt like that. She knew that he carried the weight of the world on his shoulders.

Monique eased the door shut to the bathroom as the dense steam engulfed her. She could see the shadow of Rasheed's nude body as he showered. She quickly undressed and opened the shower stall door. Rasheed stood under the water with his eyes closed with a bar of soap in one hand and a washcloth in the other.

He must have felt a draft because he opened his eyes just as she stepped into the shower with him. Her nubile breasts gently brushed against his stomach, causing him to inhale her feminine scent. She looked like a midget standing next to a giant as she stared up at him. The water ran as the steam fogged them in a hue of gray. Monique searched for the right words to fill the void of love's passion that was missing from their relationship. On tiptoes she leaned forward and kissed his nipple.

"Ra," she spoke. Her delicate voice echoed in the backdrop of torrential waters. "You're my man, my king, my everything."

She gently began to rub his muscular chest, his six-pack abs.

"Mo, you think I should have kicked his ass?"

"Shh …" she whispered, placing her finger over his lips, feeling the two-day stubble of a beard on her wrist.

She reached down and held his manhood, which responded to her gentle touch. He closed his eyes and allowed her sultry voice to relax him as the hot, torrid water tranquilized him, relieving all the pent-up anger and frustration like a knotted rope being released from around his neck. A protracted sigh escaped from his lips.

"You like this? Does this feel good?" Monique cajoled in a husky, seductive voice as she stroked him, causing him to relinquish a part of himself that will forever be a woman's true conquest—his body.

"Remember when I asked you if I could make love to you?" she asked in a breathy voice, whispering against his skin as the water drenched her face.

The fahrenheit only seemed to increase as she deftly continued to stroke him with both hands, rubbing his penis on her erect nipples. Her lubricious tongue began an exploration across his wide, brawny chest, tasting the sweet taste of his brown skin like he was molasses.

She sucked on his nipple, feeling it grow hard on the tip of her tongue, causing him to shudder and moan. Her mouth traveled down south leaving a trail of hot saliva to be erased by the waters that bathed them. She made a stop at his belly button. She now held his enormous penis in both hands as she primed him with even strokes, feeling the thick veins that ran along the shaft.

Gently he placed both of his large hands on her shoulders, a silent gesture beckoning her, willing her. His body quivered. Finally, just about when he felt he could not take any more, she slowly got down on her knees. Stroking him, she gently kissed the head of his member. He was hard as a rock. She meant just what she had said when she asked him if she could make love to him.

Her love was the only thing a black woman could give freely when all else failed and reconciliation was the only form of redemption. Slowly her tongue rode the head of his penis then down the long sleek surface as she leaned back against the wall, taking him with her. A towel fell in the water as she drew him in her mouth, causing him to exhale deeply. She slowly deep-throated him, letting him fill her completely as she bobbed her head up and down … up and down … lips and tongue sucking and massaging with warmth from her mouth.

Her saliva lubricated him, willing him to deposit his seed deep within her throat. Her rhythm quickened with a fervid intensity. Loud slurping, sucking noises resonated as she devoured as much of him as her mouth would allow. He palmed her head gently and groaned with pure ecstasy at the feel of her mouth. Her hand manipulated his balls, gently tugging at them. The rhythm grew faster, almost on the fringe of a fanatical climax, causing him to moan.

He was ready to explode with an enormous orgasm. Monique held on to his penis with both hands and sucked greedily. He lost control as he cursed God and called to Jesus with what felt like oceans of jet streams filling her mouth. Getting his dick sucked had never felt so good in his entire life. Then she pulled away, leaving him to dangle as a dribble of cum glistened off her pursed bottom lip.

A tuft of matted hair stuck to her face and eyes as the water splashed her body. Ever so gently, Rasheed wiped at the water obscuring her face and eyes. He wondered, as men seldom do, why his woman was going through such great lengths to please him. He knew her knees had to hurt and she also had just gotten her hair done.

Monique smiled up at him starry-eyed as his penis dangled in front of her face. She blinked back the water and caressed him one more time as she took him back in her mouth and hummed. She used all the force in her jaw muscles to stimulate him with her tongue. A young girl can learn a lot from X-rated movies. And indeed she had.

She pulled her mouth away from him again. This time he asked in a croaked, strained voice full of passion, "What's wrong?"

She ignored him like she was in a world of her own. She caressed his penis, enjoying the feeling of controlling his lust for her, the feeling that only a real woman felt when she had really mastered the art of loving her man, causing him to crave her, need her, long for her in such a way that only she suffices.

She rubbed the head of his penis on her breasts, savoring the moment for when she planned to have him deep inside of her. With his hardened shaft between her breasts, she squeezed them together, causing him to whisper words that not even he understood. She stood and turned the water off. Her firm pendulous breasts bounced, her quarter-sized nipples aimed at him.

She took his hand, soaking wet as they padded from the bathroom, leaving a trail of water behind, along with their inhibitions.

The baby lay at the end of the bed asleep. They were careful not to disturb him. This would not be their first time stealing love while the baby slept in the same bed.

Monique gently placed the condom on Rasheed as he sat on the bed, leaning back on his elbows. She smiled to herself. His penis looked like a crooked light pole.

Monique whispered, "You know you're going to have to go slow with me. I wanna ride it."

He nodded his head as she stood in front of him. He watched the lovely patch of hair between her legs. It looked like she was trying to hide a small monkey.

"Remember, I'm making love to you, my king," she whispered with a twinkle in her eyes, as succulent beads of water cascaded off her body.

His throat was thick with passion as again, he bobbed his head as he listened to his woman's sweet command. Slowly she mounted him like she was climbing a mountain. He lay back on the bed and watched. With his latexed penis she spread the lips of her vagina and eased the head in slowly.

From his vantage point, the view was great. Monique was positioned like a jockey on a horse as she slid a painful inch in and made a face that he knew all too well. He had no choice but to aid her. Even though she desperately wanted to make love to him, she was too tight –actually, he was too large. That depended on who you asked. With her heat smothering him he humped in a deep upward thrust, so deep that it felt like she could feel him in her chest cavity. She moaned and groaned as she thrashed her head from side to side.

He palmed her ass and went deeper, causing her eyes to roll to the back of her head as her body French kissed his. He continued to palm her ass, squeezing it, guiding, controlling her like a rag doll as he plunged deeper, faster, seizing control of what should have been her dominance over him, all for the benefit of giving him her love. She wanted to ride him to that place of pure ecstasy, but his thrusts turned almost violent as he moved inside of her using her body like she was a joystick.

In the fitful pounding, he pulled her down on him, filling her with all eleven inches. It felt like she was being torn in half as her supple breasts bounced in the air. She held onto his hairy chest and repressed a scream as his pace quickened. A slippery sound of flesh resonated as her body was heaved up and down with so much force she no longer had any control over his wanton lust.

"Ra … sheed … stop … you're … you're … hurting meee," she droned as he continued to pound away inside of her like some crazed maniac.

Her body bounced in the air. Finally, he exploded in convulsions as he pressed her vagina tight against his body and cursed as the ebb and flow of love-making finally subsided.

Exhausted, her body collapsed to his side, her right leg on top of his left. His panting echoed throughout the room as his muscles began to relax.

He thrust one more time for the sake of having a semi-hard erection. Monique began to move with his slow strokes inside of her. He assumed the position on top which forced her legs to open wide. He watched as he slid in and out of her slippery opening, still not fully erect. Monique loved his fervid passion when it grew weak like now, as long as he was still hard. She closed her eyes, enraptured. Her sex was strange; it was always hard for her to achieve an orgasm, but then tears spilled over onto her cheeks as he slowly moved inside of her, not as a beast, but as a lover.

She began to cry tenderly, lovingly, as he looked at her confused. Tears? She read his mind and smiled through her tears and shivered. "It feels sooo good. You feel so good inside of me. Oh God, please just go slow … like that, yeah … yeah …" She had awakened something inside of him, but now he was the aggressor.

Then it happened. As she opened her mouth to scream to the heavens, another cry of terror caused them to both turn and look.

Lil' Malcolm was wide awake, his doe eyes filled with fear as he stared and pointed at his father with his little stubby fingers.

"You hurtin' mommy," he cried.

Rasheed quickly pulled out of Monique and dived under the covers.

"What's wrong, lil' man?" Rasheed asked his son.

Monique giggled under the covers. He turned and glowered at her as she pulled the cover down to her chin, smiling, satiated from sex as only a woman can describe.

"You hurt mommy," Malcolm said, causing Monique to laugh.

Rasheed threw a pillow at her. She ducked, placing the covers over her face as her body continued to rock with jubilant spasms of laughter.

Women! Rasheed thought as he tore his eyes away from her.

"No, Malcolm, daddy was not hurting mommy. I was making love to her," he said affectionately.

"Don't tell him that!" Monique said, popping her head from under the covers.

"What you want me to tell him?" Rasheed asked, making a face at her. "I sure as hell ain't fitna lie to him about the birds and the bees, so he can come home at thirteen telling us that he got his twelve-year-old girlfriend knocked up or worse."

He turned back to his son, "Come here, lil' man." The child sniffled and crawled into his father's arms. "I wasn't hurting mommy. Watch this," he chimed playfully as he leaned forward and kissed Monique on her lips.

Surprisingly, she reached up, grabbing both of them in a hug. Malcolm squealed with delight, wedged between his loving parents as they both tickled and smothered him with kisses until his belly hurt from laughing. Moments afterward, Rasheed and Monique dozed off to sleep.

Malcolm stealthily eased out of the bed and rambled through the house until he found Grandma Hattie in the kitchen cooking breakfast.

Thirteen

Jack the Ripper

The luxurious platinum package, limited-edition Mercedes had a customized front grill. The inside was handsomely decorated in black leather and sheepskin with a host of gadgets found throughout. The state of the art Alpine stereo system thumped so hard that it vibrated the ground. Quiet as it's kept, within the car's interior design was a hide-away compartment, especially designed to conceal guns and drugs.

Jack Lemon sat comfortably in the passenger seat with the air conditioner blowing, one hand on his pistol and the other on Gina's thigh. The smoldering smoke from the blunt wedged between his lips made him snarl as he tried to keep the smoke out of his eyes. A sense of satisfaction enveloped Jack and he smiled as he thought about Damon's decapitated body. An example of what happens to snitch niggas. He wondered how long it would be before they found him.

Monique staggered from the bed to the sound of loud music outside the window. She strained her eyes against the sunlight as she looked at the clock on the nightstand next to the bed, 1:28 PM. She groggily rose from the bed, placing her feet on the wooden floor. She looked out the window and saw the large automobile gleaming in the ardent sunlight. She couldn't tell who was inside because of the dark tinted windows. Then she looked around.

"Malcolm?" She called his name. Rasheed stirred in his sleep.

One of his long legs came out from under the covers. It reminded her of the sex they had. She was sore down there. She put on Rasheed's T-shirt and headed for the door. On her way out, she glanced in the mirror.

I look like shit, she thought, as she brushed her hair down with her hand. The potent scent of their love-making was still in the air, or was it just her?

On the kitchen table she found a note from Grandma Hattie.

It said that she and Malcolm went grocery shopping with Aunt Esta. There was a knock at the door. As she padded her way through the living room, she once again patted at her nappy hair as she opened the door thinking about her ruined relaxer.

She was surprised to see Jack standing there. He had a shit-eating grin on his face.

"Jack Lemon!" She smiled broadly, happy to see him, while at the same time regretting she had come to the door looking like a real chicken head.

Once again she mopped at her hair with her hands. He hugged her and laughed. He smelled like a marijuana factory and, painfully, that reminded her of his criminal past. They had been friends since high school, but it was mostly because of Rasheed. Jack was Jack. He loved to flirt with death, amongst other things.

"Did you get the money I gave Ra to give to you?" he asked.

She nodded and cast a glance out the door and looked back at him. "Whose car is that and how did you get out of prison? They said you had life in the feds." She delivered a rapid fire of words.

If Jack was anything, he was trouble in the worst way.

"Damn shawty, why the twenty questions? Yeah, that's my whip," he nodded nonchalantly toward the car. "A nigga doing big thangs. I'm fitna put this thang on mash! Shit gonna be different this time."

"Really," she said, curling her lips as she arched her brow.

"Where that nigga Ra at? I told him I was gonna take him shoppin'."

She drew in a deep breath. "J, Rasheed's asleep and he told me not to wake him up for nobody," she lied.

Her gut was telling her to protect her man. Jack was cool, but she knew that he was up to no good. She needed to express this to him in such a way as to not offend him, but let him know what was up.

"We got a three-year-old son now." She tried to smile.

"I know, he sent me pictures of y'all when I was in."

"No, you don't know, Jack," she said with calm emphasis. "I love you like crazy, but you're the reason that Rasheed was not able to go to a major college. He might have even been in the NBA by now."

"Me?" Jack huffed, pointing a finger at his chest.

"Yeah, you. The last time you came 'round here in a new car, it was stolen and Rasheed took the fall for it."

Jack exploded. "Bullshit! We rented a car from a crackhead. I gave him six rocks to rent it for the entire day. Later that day I went to the store to buy some beer. We didn't know that junkie had reported the car stolen. I came out the store, five-O all over the car. They found the weed and the burner in the car. What could I do?" Jack threw both of his hands up.

Monique shook her head. She had nothing against Jack, but, damn.

"The next thing I know, the shit was all on the news and in the papers."

"Jack, please just understand what I'm sayin'. I got mad love fo' ya, that's word, but you're gonna end up dead or back in the joint if you don't change."

"I ain't never going back to the joint," Jack said with a dead serious expression on his face as he adjusted the gun on his waist. "I'ma be a'ight this time. I'm a seven figga nigga now, Ma. I ain't gotta grind no mo' if I don't want to. Know what I mean?"

A car horn blew. Monique strained her eyes as she looked out the door at the female getting out the car.

"Gina!" Monique recognized her old friend. They had not seen each other in years.

"Gina Thomas, girrrl, come here!" Monique hollered with glee, causing Jack to make a face as he placed his fingers in his ears.

All that damn yelling like they still cheerleaders, he thought. Gina went inside the house. The two women danced jubilantly as they exchanged hugs. She was wearing a fly Baby Phat blue pantsuit that accentuated all her curves, giving her ample cleavage the attention it deserved. She wore a pair of Versace sandals to match her purse.

Rasheed came in the room with a look on his sleepy face wondering what all the commotion was all about. He took one look at Gina and Monique hugging in the middle of the floor and smiled as he scratched his privates and yawned. He wore a sheet around him like it was a toga.

"What's up son?" Rasheed said, stifling a yawn.

"Mo was just telling me that she was 'bout to wake you up," Jack said as he cut his eyes at Monique. She made a face at him.

They all talked for a minute then the girls went into the kitchen to fix the guys something to eat.

Once the girls had left, Jack said to Rasheed, "Mo still got a little hate in her blood for me."

"Yeah, kinda, but that shit go back to high school since the day we ran a train on Sha-Sha at Brenda's party."

"B, her pussy smelled like rotten fish and some mo' shit," Jack chuckled, causing Rasheed to crack up in laughter as he walked over to the front door, opening it.

The system in the Benz was so loud that Rasheed could feel it reverberating under his feet.

"Daaamn, whose whip you done stole this time?" Rasheed droned, half serious.

The car was beautiful. It must have cost over a hundred grand. As Jack reached into his pocket, Rasheed noticed a platinum and diamond Rolex watch on his wrist. Jack pulled out a small black device about the size of a pack of cigarettes. He pushed a button and the stereo system's music lowered. They could hear the girls in the kitchen rattling pans and gossiping like schoolgirls as they laughed.

"Damn, Gina looks good, son. What happened to the bracelets and ponytails she used to wear back in the day?" Rasheed asked.

"Kid, she doing her own thug thizzal now-a-days. Straight gangstress. When I took her out the house she was a foot dragger with potential. Now, she's a thoroughbred, game tight."

Rasheed pulled at the sheet around his waist as he listened to his friend. The front room of his grandma's house was cluttered with all kinds of trophies and plaques. Jack reached up and caressed a gold ball atop a trophy that stood almost six feet tall, trophies that went back to when Rasheed played junior basketball at seven years old.

Guilt-ridden, Jack wondered for the umpteenth time, if he hadn't gotten that car from that junkie that day, would Rasheed be now playing in the pros? He, along with everybody else, knew the answer to that. Like some invisible demon, the two never talked about it, they always managed to walk around the subject. In his heart it pained Jack miserably and he had sworn to himself, if it was the last thing he ever did, he would make amends with his friend.

"Think fast!" Jack said, tossing Rasheed a wad of money wrapped in a rubber band. The sheet almost fell off of him as he grabbed the money out of the air and gave Jack a facial expression that read, 'what's this for?'

"Nigga, we fitna go splurge Jack the Ripper style." He then added, "That's twenty G's, stack it like you like it." Rasheed felt the corners of his cheeks pull back into a smile. "Nigga, is you tryna roll to the lot for a new whip or not?"

Rasheed scratched his head as he vaguely heard the women in the kitchen.

Monique stepped into the doorway. "Food ready!" her voice sang. She knotted her brow, grimacing at the money in

Rasheed's hand. "Baby, can I see you in the bedroom for a sec?" She tried to keep the disgruntled apprehension out of her voice.

Once they entered the room she snapped. "Don't you let that nigga get you in trouble."

He spun around and grabbed her shoulders. "I don't care what you say. You ain't never liked none of my friends."

"That's a lie." She frowned as she pulled away from him. She took a step back and stretched, arching her back like a cat.

"Personally, I don't have nothing against Jack. I just don't want him to get you in trouble again. All this money, Ra … it just feels like he's trying to buy your friendship," she said in a small voice as she turned away from him. He thought he saw tears in her eyes.

"Ma, I'm going to be okay." With that he went to take a shower. Afterward, they ate breakfast together. The girls exchanged numbers and Rasheed left with Jack and Gina. Monique declined to go.

Rasheed picked out a Cadillac SUV with expensive 22-inch rims. He had other accessories added to the car like tint, a customized grill and another DVD player especially for Malcolm. The dealership owner asked them to come back the following Monday. They had to take extra precaution with the paper work since the vehicle was paid for in cash. They didn't need the feds sneaking around.

As they drove away, Jack thought he detected something in Gina's eyes – jealousy. As Rasheed rode in the back seat, he noticed all the fine handmade oak craftsmanship that went into the design of the car. There was a bar, two telephones – one on each side of the car – and televisions in the headrests. Rasheed looked down at the floor. Wedged in the front seat was a chrome-plated nine. His heart leapt in his chest, pounding so hard he could hardly breathe.

He leaned back in his seat. That's when he saw the pound of weed inside a Ziploc bag. It had a purple tint to it. Gina saw his expression in the rearview mirror and danced her eyebrows at Jack to get his attention. Jack turned around and saw something in his friend's eyes—fear.

"Son, I could have put the brink and burner in the stash spot, but I learned when a nigga riding dirty and them folks pull a nigga over with the K-9 unit, I can just get out and run." He reached back and hit Rasheed on the leg reassuringly. "Son, I promise you, I'm never goin' to let you get fucked up again." Gina suddenly put on the brakes at the stoplight, causing Jack to jerk forward. He shot her a glare that said 'what the fuck you doing?'.

Jack continued, "Besides, I ain't even gonna front. I been in this grimy-ass city too long, seen to many niggas get caught slippin'. I'd rather get caught with my heat than without it."

Rasheed nodded his head and swallowed the lump in his throat. In the back of his mind he could hear Monique's voice, like some evil incantation.

Moments later, they dropped the drugs off at an old, run-down house that Gina had rented in Coney Island. Afterward, they decided to ride through their old stomping grounds in BK, flaunting the luxury car. They were drinking Hennessy and Coke as Jack puffed on a large blunt. He had the burner under his seat as they all exchanged war stories and laughed. The atmosphere was relaxed as they rode along getting high off blunts and drunk on nostalgic memories.

The night was alive and vibrant in New York City, the hub of the world. Gina drove, Jack navigated, telling her where to turn, what dope hole to visit. This was the part of the game that Gina loved. Jack Lemon was that nigga and just about every spot they stopped, cats showed love to him by giving him cash. It wasn't no military secret, Jack was the nigga you wanted on your team.

Niggas broke bread out of love and some did it as a way to renew their payments on protection fees. Jack Lemon was back out. To some, that was mind-boggling, because many hated him, most feared him, but all respected him.

Damn, it feels good to be a gangsta,Jack thought as they rode around, bending corners in the Benz. Shit was looking lovely, even by his standards.

He glanced over at Gina as she snapped her fingers, jamming to the music on the radio, going to that place where women go when they're truly relaxed, looking sexy and don't even know it.

DJ Clue stopped the music and began to speak in a somber tune.

"To all my hip-hop fam out there, G-Solo and Big Prophet just walked into the studio."

"Yo … yo … what's up, son?" Prophet and G-Solo said in chorus as chairs and microphones could be heard moving around in the background.

DJ Clue continued, "It's really an honor to have these two double-platinum-selling artists in the station." After the small formalities ended, DJ Clue spoke to the listeners. "Everyone listen up, this is important. There's a hundred thousand dollar reward for the whereabouts of Damon Dice of DieHard Records."

"Hold up!" Jack said, throwing up his hand, spilling his drink on his pants and on the seat.

Gina turned her head and glanced at Jack. Like hers, his expression was intense as he wrinkled his brow in concentration, listening to the radio.

"This is for all the heads out there that have been supporting DieHard Records." G-Solo was talking. "My man Damon Dice was abducted the other night. As usual, the police ain't tryna do $%&* about it." The radio station bleeped out the curse word.

"However, they do say that foul play is suspected. That's bull#*%$ 'cause we know for sure that at the time of his abduction the police had Damon under surveillance, and they let this atrocity happen right under their noses. Now we're offering a one-hundred-thousand-dollar reward for any information, no matter how small it may be, as long as it helps us find him."

DJ Clue cut in, "I hear that y'all have a significant lead already."

"Yeah, yeah, a bitch hit him up." The station wasn't quick enough to bleep that out. "She got a tattoo on her breast of either an apple or an orange. It could even be a lemon with the initials J.L. or J.M. underneath it. I can't be too sure 'cause we was all drinkin' that night."

Jack bolted straightforward in his seat and looked at Gina's breast. Her clothes concealed her tattoo. From the back seat,Rasheed watched their reaction.

Could Jack have abducted Damon Dice? Rasheed wondered. He thought about the blood on Jack's pants and his most recent purchase of a handsaw and cement.

Rasheed gulped down the rest of his drink.

Big Prophet was on the mic talking now. "She followed us from the club to the hotel. That's when I saw her again, in front of the hotel lobby with Damon. Sometime after that, he was abducted at gunpoint and placed in the trunk of a car, and the whole time, the police just sat around watching."

"We already got the mysterious deaths of Biggie and Pac," DJ Clue reminded the listeners. "Not to mention Jam Master Jay, God rest their souls. What is it that our listeners can do to help?"

"Somebody out there has seen something. This same chick picked up a large sum of money at Damon's mom's crib. We can't be sure that it was her, but I got a gut feelin' it was. Also, we're pretty sure she got into a high-speed chase with the police and they let her get away."

Jack Lemon grinded his teeth as he disdainfully listened to Big Prophet. The same nigga that used to sit in the courtroom smiling and laughing with Damon Dice when the rat was on the stand lying on him.

Jack slammed his fist into the dashboard. Gina cringed. Jack remembered the big man smiling and exchanging daps with Damon Dice when the judge pronounced a life sentence and the officers led him away in shackles to die in prison.

"So, if y'all saw the woman again do you think you could pick her out of a lineup?" The radio host asked.

"Hell yeah!"

"Damn right!" The two men answered in unison.

"It's these coward-ass niggas these days that put they bitches on the front line to do all they dirty work," Big Prophet offered in a thick baritone voice dripping with venom.

"Personally, I believe it's a nigga in BK somewhere. Anyway, son, I got a message for you," G-Solo challenged. "When I get my hands on your bitch's ass, whoever it was that set this whole thing up, I'ma punish you, bad. Yeah, I'm putting you on blast, 'J,' whatever your name is."

Visibly shaken, Gina pulled over to the side of the road. Rasheed sat in the back seat, stiff as a board, with a fresh drink in hand. Earlier he was sitting in the back seat plotting how he was going to sneak to Monique's job to see how she really earned all that money. Now he was racking his brain trying to remember what kind of tattoo Gina had on her chest. He knew better than to open his mouth. Something had gone down, and it had something to do with Damon Dice, the man who had testified against Jack.

"Move over! I'm driving," was all Jack said. He had that glassy look in his eyes that she knew all too well. Murder, murder, murder was the theme that rang in his head as he got into the driver's seat.

Jack did a U-turn in the middle of the street. They listened as a caller called in. He had a heavy foreign accent. To their utter shock he said that an attractive female came into his jewelry store.

He went on to describe the tattoo on Gina's breast and what she looked like to a T.

"The woman told me that her old man had just gotten out the joint and she wanted something really nice for him. So I told her a Rolex would be nice. She had me inscribe 'G loves J.L.' on the back of the watch."

"Did you get her name and number?" Prophet asked with excitement in his voice.

"Yes, but it's at the store," the caller offered. "I'm at home now. I just so happened to be turning the radio station and I heard you asking about this woman."

Jack glared at Gina as he drove.

"I'm sorry," she mouthed quietly with a fearful look on her face. They both listened as the man gave the address to his establishment.

"First thing in the morning, I'm going to see dude. A jewelry store, huh?" Jack said aloud, talking to no one in particular as he drove with both hands on the steering wheel.

"I'ma hafta drop you off at the crib. Somethin' just came up," Jack snapped over his shoulder as he turned down the radio.

Rasheed nodded his head in the dark as he looked out the window watching the world go by. He knew what Jack was about to do. Rasheed's thoughts went back to the blood on Jack's pant legs. He took another sip from his drink and leaned back in his seat. Shit!

As Jack turned down 4th Avenue, the block that Rasheed's grandma lived on, he noticed an unmarked Caprice pull up behind him. Jack had the pistol in his lap. The unmarked car was all on his rear bumper. Furtively, he passed Gina the burner. She placed it in the hidden compartment.

"You a'ight?" Rasheed asked from the back seat as they pulled into the driveway.

"Yeah, the po-po right behind us. Hold that drink down."

Rasheed turned around and saw Lieutenant Brown getting out of his car. He walked up and tapped on the driver's window. Jack lowered it slowly. Brown fanned the air as the scent of weed drifted from the car window into the gray haze of the streetlights.

Lieutenant Brown did a double take at seeing Jack behind the wheel of such an expensive car.

"Hot damn! Jack Lemon. How in the hell did you get out?"

"They slipped, I gripped, same ole', same ole'. You know how it goes," Jack said nonchalantly as he popped his collar.

They were having the traditional cops and robbers dialogue. Brown ducked his head down to get a better look into the car. He saw Gina in the passenger's seat. She had her arm on the armrest with her hand poised under her chin. Her manicured fingernails glistened as she rubbed her chin.

"Hello, young lady," Brown said. She didn't answer.

One thing that Lieutenant Brown had to admit, Jack Lemon was a seasoned hustler and maybe even a cold-blooded killer. Even a police lieutenant was forced to respect that.

"What, it's your turn to beat me this time?" Rasheed questioned sarcastically, reminding Brown of the situation the night before between him and Officer Tate.

"Listen Ra, that officer was reprimanded. Why don't you let that go?"

"Like hell," Rasheed retorted as he got out the car, his height towering over the lieutenant.

"One day you'll find out I'm one of the good guys. It's going to take black police officers to stop white police brutality."

"Yeah, and what is it going to take to stop black cops from doing more harm to their own race than white cops?"

Lieutenant Brown, lost for words, stood there and looked at Rasheed.

"One of the worst things in the world they can do is give a nigga a job overseeing his own kind. He worse than a cracka."

"You need to let that go," the lieutenant said again, with steel in his voice.

Rasheed refused to back down. "My grandma helped raise you. You used to talk all that black power junk." He looked at Jack and continued, "This nigga went to school with your old man."

"Chill, nigga," Jack said, frowning with just enough of a hint to remind Rasheed there was a gun in the car.

The front porch lights came on. Monique walked out. She had her hair re-done. It reminded Rasheed that he was going to sneak to her job that night and watch the show.

"Just because I'm a cop doesn't mean that I don't understand the plight of my people. I promise you one of these days you're going to find that out. Oh, and by the way, one of the reasons I was tailing you was because the light over your license plate is out. That's reason enough for a routine traffic stop," he spoke and raised his eyebrows. "Better me than them." Lieutenant Brown smiled, knowing they got his point. "Y'all have a nice day … and Jack, get that light fixed." Jack nodded his head at Lieutenant Brown as he walked back to his patrol car.

Jack turned to Rasheed, "Man, you gotta learn how to finesse dude."

"Fuck 'em!" Rasheed said, walking up to Jack, giving him a dap. "Be careful, man."

With that, he walked away to let Jack go handle his business. Jack got back into his car, turned up the stereo and exited the driveway.

G-Solo and his bodyguard, Big Prophet, left the radio station in somewhat of a hurry after DJ Clue was immediately called into the program manager's office. He knew he was going to get reprimanded for the language the two exhibited a few moments ago.

Once they exited the building, they stood in silence. It was one of those starless Saturday nights with a full moon in the sky, and the air was beginning to turn cool. They were thankful, for once, that there weren't any groupies waiting outside the radio station.

The parking lot was small, for security purposes. A few cars dotted the parking lot as they headed for the Maybach limousine parked a few feet away. The motor was idling as they got into the car.

G-Solo picked up the car phone. "Steve, drop Prophet off at the club first, then you can take me home to Jersey." A grumbled reply came from the other end of the phone as the car pulled onto the streets.

"Listen, whoever this chick is, I promise you I'ma find her." Prophet was continuing their conversation.

"I dunno, I got a bad vibe about this whole thing. You heard what dude said back there at the radio station. He compared

Damon's kidnapping to Biggie and Pac. Besides, Damon used to say it himself, the mob had their hands in about 90% of the rap game."

"That's bullshit! All we gotta do is find this red bitch with the tattoo on her chest. Money talks. I betcha for a hundred G's that hoe's own mama would drop a dime," Prophet said in an attempt to console G-Solo.

G-Solo frowned and said, "Then how in the hell does a nigga like him get kidnapped when he got mo' police 'round him than the President? Dude was s'pose to be under surveillance."

"I can't answer that, but my man that works at the police station pulled my coat, told me keep it on the lo-lo, but Damon was working with the Chief of Police, cat by the name of Brooks. Some kind of way they had a fallout, and the cop had a hair up

his ass for Damon."

"Damon workin' for the police? Man, I don't believe that shit!" G-Solo shook his head in disbelief and slumped in his seat.

"Hey, I'm just telling you what was told to me by a good source."

They rode in silence for a moment as they both considered what to do.

"Did you see the way the phones lit up back there at the station? Dude that called in said he owned the jewelry store—that's our man," Prophet said reassuringly as he watched G-Solo slump further into his seat.

One thing was for damn sure, G-Solo had no intentions of ever taking the lead. He was a follower. They both knew that with the looming possibility of Damon Dice being dead,

DieHard Records was in serious trouble. Even though G-Solo rapped about being a gangster – his money, his hoes, his cars and his clothes – personally, he had never lived this lifestyle. He came from a middle-class family and attended Catholic school.

Suddenly the limousine came to a stop. "Where the fuck we at?" Big Prophet yelled, looking out the window into the pitch black darkness.

The window divider that separated the chauffeur from the passengers opened. A woman wearing a New York baseball cap, ponytail and dark shades stuck her head in the window and announced tersely, "Somebody said you was lookin' fo' me."

The red beam from the .44 bounced around off the two men's foreheads as it ominously stabbed at the darkness until it finally settled on Big Prophet's forehead.

"Oh shit!" G-Solo screeched as they both recognized the woman at the same time. The door opened next and a masked gunman got inside the car. Everything was moving fast as both men looked on, startled.

"Big man, you like to rap a lot. Just be careful what you ask fo'," Jack said as he pressed his nine-millimeter against Prophet's throat while at the same time relieving him of the gun under his coat.

"Wha … wha … the fuck's going on?" Prophet stuttered.

Jack sat down opposite of both men, his composure dangerously cool and calm. "Bitch-made nigga, you gonna go on the radio and sell death to me," Jack said with a menacing scowl on his face, his voice sounding like dry ice being dragged across a wooden floor.

"Man, I don't even know you," Prophet responded, his voice hinting at a plea.

"Aw, nigga, you know me. I'm the nigga you was looking fo' You called me out, so I'm here, J.L. in the flesh."

His neck snapped back like he had been slapped when he realized who was sitting across from him with a gun leveled at his head.

"Listen, man, I ain't got nothing against nobody," Prophet said, knowing that the first real law of the streets was to never buck a jack.

"Take whatever you want," G-Solo said timidly as he took off his Rolex. For some reason, G-Solo focused all of his attention on Gina as she moved the beam in intervals, dancing it off both men's foreheads.

"You ain't gotta tell me that," Jack said, aiming the gun at G-Solo. "I plan to take what I want. And since your man here," he pointed the gun at Prophet, "got a slick-ass mouth, he just earned himself a closed casket. I'ma dress your punk ass up."

"Hold up, man! Hold up! I didn't mean no harm," the big man said with his palms raised in the air. G-Solo cowered next to him.

"I didn't say nothin'," G-Solo chimed in somberly. All the manliness was gone from his voice. He almost sounded feminine, on the verge of tears.

"Both of y'all shut the fuck up," Jack said.

Silence.

"You might have a chance," Jack said to G-Solo, pointing the gun in his direction. "But you, fat boy," Jack spoke to Prophet, "this is your only chance."

He reached into his pocket and removed a large water pistol. "Nigga, I'ma let you choose your weapon of death, which is better than the chance you gave me."

Prophet looked at Jack, narrowing his eyes at him and said, "What, you crazy or somethin'?"

Jack smirked as he calmly aimed the real gun at Prophet's kneecap and fired. The blast from the gun was deafening in the small confines of the car.

The big man hollered. "Aw shit, aw shit, you fuckin' shot me!"

He grabbed his knee with a face stricken with both pain and terror as he looked at the madman sitting across from him. The red beam from the light continued to tease his mind as it roamed across his face and eyes. G-Solo whimpered as he looked on with his hands clasped in prayer.

"Okay, I'ma ask you one mo' time, and this time be careful how you respond. Know what I mean?"

Prophet grimaced in pain as he nodded his head up and down.

"Which weapon of death do you prefer?" Jack reiterated.

Prophet pointed to the water gun and croaked hoarsely, "The water gun."

How in the world can a water gun kill someone? He thought.

For the first time, Jack displayed what could have passed for a smile as he raised the water pistol, taking aim and then lowered it.

"First, let me tell you a lil' joke."

Gina sucked her teeth impatiently. Jack knew he had made the wrong decision in bringing her, but he would deal with her later. She rolled her eyes at him and let the smoked glass divider separate them while Jack continued with his business.

"Where was I? Oh, the joke," he said as if talking to himself.

Prophet moaned, holding what was left of his shattered kneecap.

"Ever heard any of them white man, Chinese man, black man jokes?" Jack Lemon asked, his voice sounding sinister as he continued looking out the window.

No answer.

He pointed the gun at Prophet's other knee. "Nigga, you hard of hearin' or somethin'?

"No, no please!" Prophet begged as he covered his good knee with his hands and pushed his back against the car door.

G-Solo looked on with fear-filled eyes. In an attempt to distance himself from his wounded friend, he slid his body as far away as the limited space would allow. He mumbled something about the Lord being his shepherd. Again, Jack furtively glanced out the window.

The muffled sounds of the chauffeur screaming in the trunk disturbed Jack. The man had promised to be quiet. Jack made a mental note to blow a hole in the trunk of the car before he departed.

"Okay, there was this African king," Jack said rhythmically, causing his voice to fluctuate in tune as he reached over and started squirting Prophet in the face with the water pistol. "The big black king's name was Mutoto. He was the most feared king in all of Africa." Jack glanced out the window again. "He had a harem of beautiful women that lived not too far from the village. Three men from the village had got caught sneaking into the harem. They had been sexing the king's wives. So, his loyal servants brought one of the men before the king. This was the Chinese man. The king asked, 'Boungy or death?'—Boungy meaning that a big, black Mandingo African would bend the little Chinese man over and fuck him in the ass with a two-foot dick or else choose death. The little Chinese man happily chose Boungy." Jack snickered like the Devil himself at his own crude joke as he squirted Prophet with the water gun.

"Next was the white man. The king asked him, 'Boungy or death?' 'Boungy,' the white man said, happy to walk away with his life." Jack continued to squir t the water pistol as they looked at him, sure that he was insane. "Last was the black man. He was all cool and shit, walked with a pimpish limp. The king asked, 'Boungy or death?' The black man frowned and said, 'Fuck you, king. I muthafuckin' choose death!'

The king chuckled with amusement and said, 'Okay, that's fine with me.' He pointed at his servant and ordered, 'Boungy until death!'" Jack smiled with his eyes hooded in mischief as he leaned over again and squirted.

It then suddenly dawned on them what Jack was up to as he placed the water gun down and lit a cigarette. The perilous fumes of the gasoline thickly permeated the air. Prophet's clothes were soaked.

His eyes grew wide with fear.

"Nooo!" he screamed at the horror that was yet to come.

"Nigga, this ya Boungy, this water gun right here. You picked it as your weapon of death." Jack looked out the window again and turned back to the big man. "I told you you got a big fuckin' mouth, plus you got snitch in yo' blood." He then turned to G-Solo and stated, "Son, this thang bigger than me and you. The earth fitna shake. A lot of niggas fitna fall through the cracks, know what I mean?" Jack drawled, winking as he casually leaned over and shot Prophet's other knee.

The big man fell in a heap onthe floor, folding up like a crushed can. He writhed in pain. Jack

took the honor of squirting him in the face.

"We ... got ... to ... make sure that ... the casket stays closed," Jack said with malice as he squirted the gun, emphasizing each word.

Prophet groaned in pain on the floor. Jack now focused his attention on G-Solo. "Somebody wants you alive, people in high places. You might be the next golden boy at DieHard. That might get your bitch ass a pass. If I had it my way, you'd be dead."

Jack stopped talking for a dramatic effect. The light from the cigarette glowed in the dark. He wanted G-Solo to marinate in fear as a duet of death sang in the car – Prophet's moaning along with the chauffeur's muffled screams from the trunk of the car – a mantra of sour melodies.

Jack spoke with determination in his voice. "In order for somebody to live, somebody gotta die. You wanna live?" Jack asked G-Solo. The frightened man nodded his head vigorously.

"Take this cigarette. I want you to do your man." Jack placed the empty water gun on the seat and removed the dangling cigarette from his lips. "If you wanna live, dude gotta die," Jack said, pointing the gun at Prophet. "If you do the job right, just maybe my boss will let you hang around at Diehard and be the next golden boy."

Just then Gina slid the window down again. "We got a problem," she informed. "The police are headed in this direction."

"Fuck!" Jack cursed under the ski mask. He knew that if they suddenly drove off it would surely get them pulled over, and if they stayed, the police would look into the car. Gina got out of the car and walked right toward them.

Fourteen

The Gentlemen's Club

He watched her svelte figure as she danced on stage as beautiful as a ballerina. His palms were sweaty and for some reason he was nervous. Monique was completely nude, and for the first time in his life, Rasheed Smith had to admit, as he looked around at all the white patrons in the club, the place was extremely tasteful in terms of its handsome décor and atmosphere. It wasn't what he had imagined. All the waitresses wore cute little bunny outfits. For the most part, the women that worked there were drop-dead gorgeous. Monique was the only black person that he had seen in the entire club.

Rasheed ensconced himself in a dark booth in the back of the club. He accepted the few looks that he received when he first walked in the door, but other than that, everything was going better than he had expected.

"Hey sexy, want a table dance?" Georgia Mae asked as she sauntered up so close to him that he could see the diamonds in her belly ring as the light cast off it. She wore a royal blue transparent sarong. Her wide hips spread so far apart that he could still see parts of Monique's show through the gap in between her legs. He tilted his head up at her and smiled as the white girl intentionally blocked his view. He couldn't help but wonder when white girls started having fat asses like the bodacious one standing right in front of him. Damn!

Seductively, Georgia Mae licked the rim of her lips as she first bobbed her head, then her body and started rhythmically grinding the air. She grabbed her hair and humped her pelvis in his face causing him to lean back in his seat. She turned around and hiked up the thin material. Underneath she was nude as she bent all the way over. She made one butt cheek dance, then the other, then to his amazement, like it was on some kind of hydraulics, her ass rose and her butt cheeks clapped. She dropped to the floor, doing a split, and got back up.

"Godmuthafuckindamn!" was all Rasheed could drawl as he sat with his mouth wide open.

The white girl had lips on her kitty that looked like human lips, only smaller. She had mesmerized him and he did a poor job of playing it off. She could see the large print in his pants.

"Naw, I'm good." He smiled as he politely tried to wave her away.

She saw the light beads of sweat starting to form on his forehead. Her vanity was slightly wounded—she had never been turned down by a man before, especially a black man. She narrowed her eyes at him as she walked up closer.

"Gee, I've never seen you before," she said.

"This is my first time," he answered as his eyes, with a mind of their own, roamed her luscious body. Forcefully, he tore his eyes away from her and looked at the stage.

"First time, huh?" she said in a dreamy voice as she placed a finger in her mouth and toyed with her tongue.

He crossed his legs one over the other. Two white men walked by. They both gave Rasheed a prolonged look, nothing disrespectful, but just enough to remind him of where he was.

"Since this is your first time here, how about a free lap dance? You never know, you might get lucky," she said with all the charm she could muster as she let the thin material she was wearing slide to the floor.

She stood in front of him, pigeon-toed and bow-legged, with a heart-shaped patch of fur between her thighs.

For the first time, he noticed her round breasts, how they curved upward, firm and succulent with an amber tint. Suddenly he had the urge to reach out and touch one of them. Instead, he reached into his pocket and removed a few bills.

"Seriously, I'm a'ight." He tried to pass her the money, but she looked at him as

if she were offended by his response.

Georgia Mae's mouth smiled but her green eyes didn't as once again, he slid his eyes off her body to look behind her at Monique on stage.

"That's Fire on stage. She's hot. You like her?" she asked as she bent down to retrieve the sarong and replaced it on her body. She walked around and sat in the chair next to him at the table.

"Who?!" Rasheed asked, as he raised his eyebrows and craned his neck to hear her over the loud music.

"That's my nizzle-fo-shizzel on stage. Her real name is Monique," Georgia Mae said with a broad smile. There was raucous applause as Monique's show ended.

Men started to throw money on stage, lots of it. Rasheed knew that he had violated the sanctity of their trust by coming to the club without telling her, but his male curiosity had gotten the best of him. Rasheed felt something crawling across his thigh. It was Georgia Mae's hand. It came to rest on his penis. She squeezed it and made a face.

"Damn, baby, you're huge," she gasped in surprise.

Delicately he removed her hand. "Don't do that," he said sternly, placing emphasis in his voice. She licked her lips and frowned, making a pouting face at him like a woman who was used to having her way.

"Honey, you know what they say, once you go white yo' life will always be right," she rhymed giddily as she flirtatiously pushed her large breasts, pink nipples like missiles, directly at him.

The talkative, fly white girl had forced him to smile with her bold antics.

"Listen, the girl on the stage, you said her name was Fire?" he asked just as the waitress appeared, dressed in a low-cut black and white bunny outfit designed to show off lots of cleavage.

"Rum and Coke, please."

"Yeah, that's my girl. She got a man and a baby though." She crossed her legs. The lights dimmed as Monique started picking up money off the floor.

"I know you've been told this many times before, but you're a very handsome black man." Rasheed blushed and smiled politely as he cut his eyes away from her to the stage.

Georgia Mae was admiring his luscious, thick brown lips, his deep chiseled dimples and his skin the color of roasted pecans. She noticed his hands were large and he was tall, too. Game was determined to do everything in her power to take this black man home with her and seduce him, one way or the other.

He watched her as her jagged green eyes held him with a piercing stare. She had the most beautiful eyes he had ever seen.

"I just came here to relax and get my thoughts together," he finally said, pulling himself away from her seductive wiles.

"You say you just came to a strip club to get your thoughts together?" she reworded his statement, making it sound lame, even to him. "If that's the case, sugar, I got more bounce to the ounce."

She gave him a seductive stare, causing him to squirm in his seat.

The room suddenly felt like the temperature had risen as he mopped at his brow with the back of his hand. She was driving him crazy, sitting in front of him partially nude with her breasts displayed like proud trophies.

He took a deep breath. "The establishment don't trip when you're sitting down propositioning the customers?" This time it was her turn to laugh, vibrant and throaty.

As her head reeled back, he couldn't help but enjoy the way her pendulous breasts bounced.

She remarked spontaneously, "As long as your sexy ass is buying the drinks I can sit here as long as I want. And if you keep up the resistance it's going to be me offering you money." With that they both erupted in jubilant laughter.

He had to admit, she was funny as well as strikingly gorgeous. Her nearness made him feel vulnerable. He had never cheated on Monique in his life.

"After the show, do you wanna come home with me?" she asked.

The expression on her face had changed. She was now dead serious as she leaned forward, as if peering inside of him. Like a woman shipwrecked, she could sense this was her last chance at grabbing land. She went for it all.

"I love old school music—the Isley Brothers, Luther—I got all their CDs, plus the new ones. You like Usher?" He nodded his head like a two-year-old.

"We could snort a couple lines of coke and fuck like rabbits. I can show you a trick or two with my ass … things you ain't never experienced before. If you think I'm joking, wait for me in the parking lot for a trial run." She was desperately determined.

Georgia Mae had turned huntress and he was the hunted as she held him enthralled with her sexual charm. She reached under the table and caressed his need. She found his penis, long and hard. It made her exhale a deep sigh as she felt moistness between her thighs.

"Please, come," she paused, "home with me."

She spoke in a sultry, breathy voice, waving a pink tongue across her lips as the promise of pure ecstasy was sealed with puckered lips. She squeezed his penis, causing him to groan. She moved closer to his earlobe and whispered as she ran her hand down the length of his penis, "Do you wanna come—"

She stopped in mid-sentence as she was interrupted by someone calling her name. It was Monique.

Outside the Gentlemen's Club, three people sat in an old Ford truck. One of them was Tatyana, the Russian girl who Monique had beaten up in the club. Her face was still partially disfigured, and because of that, her career as a model was ruined.

With smoldering hate she blamed it all on Monique. She was back with vengeance on her mind and a score to settle.

Since her career had been ruined, the only work she could find dancing was at sleazy, run-down clubs in the black section of town. The patrons were all drug dealers, shady characters who preferred to pay in drugs. It wasn't long before she started experimenting with drugs—crystal meth and crack. One of the most hellish sights in the world was to see a white girl in a black world turned out on drugs, addicted and not even aware of it. The drugs had ravaged Tatyana's mind.

In the truck with her were two huge rednecks. The malodorous funk of unwashed bodies and stale cigarettes permeated the air. The old truck was littered with Budweiser beer cans and wine bottles.

"I want you to cave her face in and break both her legs so she can never dance again," Tatyana shouted, spraying the dirty window with spittle.

One of the rednecks responded, "I'm gonna whack her in the face with this hurr ball bat and Jethro gonna run her over with the truck a coupla times."

Tatyana crinkled her reconstructed nose at the man. God, he stinks, she thought. The other redneck, Jethro, snickered as he took another hit off the makeshift crack pipe made out of an antenna. His teeth were rotten. A tuft of dirty blond hair fell over his eyes. His shoulders were broad, taking up most of the room in the cab of the truck. He passed the crack pipe to Bo.

Tatyana had found the men at a Salvation Army residence for the homeless. She had promised to pay them five hundred dollars and all the crack they could smoke.

"I promise you that gurl will never work again," Bo said, taking a hit from the pipe, inhaling deeply. The dope made a crackling sound.

Tatyana smiled devilishly. "If you don't do a good job, I'm not going to pay you," she said in broken English. She looked to her left at Bo, then to her right at Jethro and continued, "If you do a really good job you can stay at my place tonight and I will personally bathe both of you." Her voice hinted at a drug-frenzied ménage à trois. Both men laughed excitedly as if she had just tossed a bone to a hungry pack of dogs.

She reached inside a plastic bag that used to contain a fifth pack of cocaine rocks. She pinched off one of the rocks, getting just a crumb just like the blacks used to do her and passed it to Bo.

"Here's another twenty dollars," she said, with surprising quickness.

Jethro grabbed the rock and at the same time he farted so loud it vibrated the seats. Together, they waited outside the club, hidden in the backdrop of darkness. It was like Tatyana had planned, dreamed of.

Now all she needed was for the black bitch to walk out.

"Please, someone open up a window," she complained as she waited patiently. The wait wouldn't be much longer.

Rasheed turned his head long enough to see Monique walking toward the audience. Thank God she hadn't seen him yet. She was now adorned in a red robe.

"Here's your chance to meet the lovely Fire," Georgia Mae said as Monique walked straight for them.

Rasheed held his breath as he slumped down in his chair.

An elderly white man stepped in front of Monique. He had a dozen red roses in his hand for her, causing her to smile brightly.

Georgia Mae rolled her eyes at Dr. Hugstible. The old man seemed to be infatuated with her, and from the looks of it, so was the handsome man sitting across from her.

"Hey! Hey! Can a girl get a break? Damn," Georgia Mae barked. "I've done everything but propose marriage to you and your eyes have been roaming ever since I sat down." She was slightly pissed by his actions, but had to admit, Monique was an attractive woman.

Finally Georgia said, "It looks like you would like to be one of her fans. I'll introduce you to her." Georgia Mae stood.

"No! No!" He raised his voice above the music for the first time as he grabbed at her arm. Too late. She was gone.

Briskly she walked to the front of the stage, almost colliding with a waitress that was balancing two trays of drinks. A few customers tried to get her attention as she reached Monique.

"Girl, I got a man as fine as Denzel Washington, with a body like Usher." Georgia Mae said enthusiastically as she leaned closer to Monique.

"I swear to God, his thang's this long." She used both of her hands to indicate how long.

They both giggled like school girls. Another woman was about to take the stage. A few men were trying to get their attention. The lights suddenly dimmed as Georgia Mae took

Monique's hand and led her to the table. It was empty. The handsome man was gone.

"I swear to God he was here a moment ago," Georgia Mae said with a frown on her face as she searched the crowd.

Rasheed walked briskly to the parking lot, ignoring the valet.

He had parked his old hoopty way in the back of the lot. The cool air made him take notice of the night breeze. His shirt was soaked.

He glanced over his shoulder and almost walked into a parked car. Talk about a close call, he thought. His ears still buzzed from the horrible music from the club. Once he reached his car he noticed the raggedy truck parked next to it, and not just that, but the awful smell that came from one of the open windows.

The three people inside the truck watched him closely. He could feel their eyes on him like a second skin. His instincts gnawed at him – a signal – just like the smell in the air told him they were smoking crack. He got in his car.

As he fumbled with his car keys he thought he heard a woman's voice yell, "Nigger!" as he pumped the gas and turned the ignition. The batmobile sputtered and coughed, but finally the car started.

He drove off with a gut feeling that something terribly wrong was about to happen.

And indeed something terribly wrong was about to happen. Georgia Mae walked into Monique's dressing room with her thoughts whirling, creating a riveting string of emotions. Even though she had never seen the handsome black man before, it was the first time in her entire life that she felt like it was love at first sight.

"Game, why you looking at me like that?" Monique asked with a half-smile as Georgia Mae came in and straddled the chair beside her.

Dreamy-eyed, Georgia Mae watched Monique take off her makeup. Georgia Mae had changed clothes. She wore simple white, low-cut jeans, a white halter top and boots with fur on the inside of them.

"I was just wondering what it feels like to be in love with a fine black man with a dick down to his knee," she said before exhaling like she was blowing out candles.

Monique turned and looked at her friend quizzically.

"Now, where did that come from?" Monique asked.

"I want to marry a black man and have his babies so bad, I don't care what people think," Georgia Mae continued, ignoring Monique's question. "If you could have seen that fine motherfucker tonight, girl." Georgia Mae hit Monique on her leg. She continued, "You should have seen him though! He was just like I like 'em, tall, dark and handsome. The last man that loved me was a black man. He took my money and turned me out on sex and drugs. Gave me my first orgasm, and it wasn't from my vagina–"

"Stop! Okay, you're getting a little too vivid here," Monique said with a halting hand in front of Game's face.

"Somebody loves you, baby … somebody loves you, baby," Georgia Mae began to sing beautifully, melodically hitting all the high notes just like Patti LaBelle.

"Girl, where did you learn to sing like that?" Monique asked, surprised.

Before Georgia Mae could reply, Monique answered for her. "Oops, I know, I know. In all the talent shows your mom used to have you in."

Georgia Mae nodded her head. "Yup, I sang that song at the Apollo Theater. I came in second place."

Old Man Smitty, the janitor, knocked on the door and stuck his head in. "Sorry to bother you ladies, but you two are the only ones left in the building. I'm just about finished with the floor."

"Okay, we'll be out in a minute," Monique said. She then hurried to get dressed while Georgia Mae sat and hummed a tune.

She gazed around the room and stopped when her eyes saw the roses Dr. Hugstible had given to Monique. She reached out and touched one of the rose petals. The image of the unnamed black man flashed through her mind. At that very moment in time, she decided she didn't care what it took, she had to have him.

Old Man Smitty walked with a bad limp, like maybe he had broken his hip at one time. Monique and Georgia Mae stood by the door and waited as he limped toward them. He had a mop in one had and a worn handkerchief in the other. He wiped his brow and placed the rag in his back pocket as he began to fumble an enormous set of keys on a ring. It looked like it must have had over a hundred keys on it.

Monique noticed the McDonald's hamburger toy on the chain. For some reason it reminded her of her son.

Outside the club, the night was still and a constellation of bright stars embellished the black sky. A light breeze played with Georgia Mae's hair as she turned to Monique.

"Call me in the morning," Georgia Mae said as she reached out to hug Monique.

Monique pulled away from her. "I'll call you. Maybe we can go shopping."

"Yeah, that would be great." They each walked to their cars parked at separate sections of the parking lot. The parking lot was almost empty except for one truck and one other car. As Monique approached her car, she fished around in her purse for her keys.

She normally walked with them out and carried a small knife concealed in her hand for protection, but tonight she didn't. As she found her keys, she attempted to open her door, but just then, someone grabbed her arm with brute strength, spinning her around.

Her key chain fell to the ground. Terrified, she looked up at what looked like the Devil himself bearing down on her, a white man. He was huge with broad shoulders, wide like a mountain. His silhouette was cut out of the darkness by the lurid moonlight.

Monique could detect a foul odor coming from the man. Her first instinct told her to kick the giant in his balls. To her right, in the darkness, another figure appeared, taller, causing her heart to slam against her ribs with panic. Her eyes darted around frantically looking for an escape. One of the men had something in his hand as he neared. It suddenly occurred to her that it was a baseball bat.

The shadows closed in.

"What do you want? Get the fuck away from me!" Monique said with her back against the car door. The man with the bat raised it, causing her mind to switch into overdrive. Fight, scream, run! Instinctively she went into fight mode.

"You must pay for what you done to me," a female voice said in broken English.

Instantly Monique recognized the voice and it sent shivers through her spine. Tatyana nudged her way between the girth of the two big men and the two finally stood eye to eye.

When Monique saw the tall Russian woman, it was hard to believe it was her. Tatyana had lost a lot of weight. Her once beautiful eyes were now gaunt slits of hate. Her cheeks were sunken and her hair was a shade of dirty blond.

"I never meant to hurt you." Monique's voice sounded like a plea, the tremor in it gave way to her riveting fear. To her right she could see the man inching toward her with the baseball bat.

"You have no fucking idea what you have done to my life, my career. Look at my face. Look!" Tatyana hollered as she spoke with a Russian accent.

Boldly, she walked up on Monique. The two women looked at each other.

"Tatyana, I swear, I was not trying to hurt you," Monique said in a small voice with her back pressed against the car door. She could feel her legs shaking.

"You lie," the Russian spat as she hauled off and slapped Monique hard across her face with so much force that it nearly knocked her down.

"Break her fucking legs. Make sure she never dance again," Tatyana commanded, pointing at Monique's legs.

Just then, a pearl-white BMW sports coupe pulled up. The tires screeched to a halt as Georgia Mae hopped out and ran over.

"Run, Monique! Run!" she yelled as she crunched low, legs extended, arms apart, waving as if her every movement was based on timing.

And it was. Bo swung the bat at her with so much velocity it made a whooshing sound in the air. Georgia Mae timed it perfectly by spreading her legs. She ducked and came back up as swiftly as a cat, and using her momentum, she kicked him in the face, causing the bat to fly out of his hand. The blow caused him to stagger then fall backward. Hard.

In that split second Monique knew she had to react. She kicked the other man in the balls with all her might. He doubled over as her actions caught him off-guard. As she drew her leg up to kick him again, she looked over and saw Georgia Mae kicking the shit out of his partner.

Tatyana screamed like a madwoman and charged toward her. With all her might, Monique kicked, scratched and fought as Tatyana ran into her like a train. Monique felt her fist connect to Tatyana's jaw. She dropped. It was then that Monique saw the big white man grab Georgia Mae from behind like she was a rag doll and slam her, head first, on the hard concrete. It made an eerie thudding sound that Monique would never forget.

Monique reached for the key chain on the ground with her knife on it. The other man was only a few feet away. He was still stunned from the blow to his testicles, but not enough to stop him from going after Monique to accomplish the mission he had come for—to break her legs, five hundred dollars and all the crack he could smoke. He grimaced in pain as he reached to pick up the bat. For big men, they were surprisingly quick. They were, in fact, young men, but both had an old appearance from too much drinking and drugs.

Tatyana, as if possessed, teetered on one knee as she tried to get back up. She screamed at the top of her lungs, "Get her!"

The big man had the baseball bat in his hands. He came at Monique. Off balance, he swung the bat at her legs. She tried to hop out of the way using her arm to ward off the blow.

Crack!

The bat hit her arm causing pain to explode throughout her body. She cried out.

Directly in front of her, Georgia Mae lay on the ground. The delicate figure of her body curved out in crimson blood as her life spilled onto the concrete. Monique held her arm as her assailant once again prepared to swing at her legs. She somehow managed to sidestep him as Tatyana stood up wearily.

Monique took off running as fast as she could. To her horror, Jethro, the younger of the two men, came after her as she ran screaming for help. She held her wounded arm at her side as if it were a package she was carrying. They were in an isolated rural area in the wee hours of the morning. No one could hear her screams as the big man chased behind her. She could hear his labored grunts as he gained on her.

"Bitch, I'ma kill yer."

Her arm was in excruciating pain. He was only a few yards away from her and gaining with each strong stride. Fear tormented her mind as she glanced back. She stumbled and fell. He was almost upon her as she scrambled to get back on her feet. The first blow landed on her buttocks. It came with so much force that she fell back down.

He was now upon her, there was nothing she could do. Her strength was depleted as perspiration poured from her forehead. Her breath fogged in the cool air. The moon was the only witness to the hideous assault on this night as it cast its gory shadow on them. She closed her eyes and said a prayer. Maybe the next blow would be to her head and it would all end painlessly. Images of her son, Malcolm, flashed in her mind. Lord, no. Not like this. Who is going to take care of my baby?

Fifteen

Jack and Gina

Jack watched as the two patrol officers neared. The damn chauffeur continued to make noise in the trunk of the car. Jack held his breath as they approached. All he could do was watch and wait. With his mind racing as to what to do, he reached over and turned up the volume on the radio. He almost slipped on the blood on the floor as both men, G-Solo and Prophet, watched him intently, searching for any possibility of escape or flaw in his character. They both heard Gina when she said the police were nearing.

"What da fuck y'all niggas lookin' at me like dat fo'? If the po-pos get hot, y'all gonna be the first muthafuckas shot. Word is bond. Ya'll goin out execution style," Jack barked, pointing the gun back and forth at them. His baritone voice was husky with the promise of death.

Once again, he strained his eyes to see Gina approaching the two officers.

The park was dimly lit. An occasional bush or tree outlined the nocturnal landscape. To her left was a garbage can, next to it was a water fountain that ran continuously. Clinched in her hand, inside her leather jacket was a Desert Eagle. Gina had cut a hole in the lining of the jacket and positioned the gun at one of the officers' chests. Her palm sweated as she approached them.

There was little doubt in her mind that if shit got out of hand, she was going to blast first. A lone car passed, the headlights streaked across the officers' faces. She was relieved that it wasn't backup.

Gina went into a spell.

"My girlfriend's pregnant! We can't find her. We've looked everywhere," Gina said as she began to cry instant tears.

"Hold on. Hold on, ma'am," the smaller of the two officers said as he raised his hand to comfort her.

She drew in a deep breath as her shoulders heaved as if she was a distraught woman trying to seize control of her emotions. A cry of despair ripped past her lips. The younger officer had rosy cheeks and the pleasant smile of a man still in his youth. His square chin and sloping forehead gave him the appearance of a much older man.

Gina would have shot him dead in a heartbeat if he acted up. The other officer was tall and astute, the older of the two. His watchful blue eyes held her with suspicion. He frowned with a knotted brow at her. Something is wrong with this woman, he thought. He just couldn't put his finger on it.

Gina detected his suspicions and turned toward him, the gun now leveled at his chest.

"You say your girlfriend's lost and you can't find her, huh?"

"Yes, yes," Gina said, now in control.

She pointed in the opposite direction of the limo parked up the street. They were about to turn in the direction she was pointing when a muffled shout resonated in the darkness. Along with it came the sound of loud music. The taller of the two officers reached for his gun and cautiously walked toward the sound of the noise. The limousine was sheathed in complete darkness up ahead, just like everything else in the park at night.

Gina cocked the gun in her pocket as she raised her voice. "Those are my babies in the car, what are you doin'?"

The younger officer turned to his partner. "Bob, a pregnant woman is missing. I think we need to call in a K-9 unit." He then turned to Gina. "Ma'am, if she has not been missing for over twenty-four hours there's not much we can do," he said with genuine sincerity in his voice.

The other officer continued to strain his ears, listening to the night noises. He turned and walked back toward them. His demeanor was impassive. Her tears did not affect him at all. "Go wait in the car with your kids, ma'am. We'll retrace your steps," the younger officer suggested with kindness. "I have a pregnant wife at home. If your friend is out here, we'll find her. Does she normally come out here alone?"

"No. She and her boyfriend had a fight," Gina responded between bouts of sobs as she turned and walked away.

The taller officer, the older of the two, called after her, "Hey, you, stop!"

Gina felt her heart pounding in her chest because she knew what was next—gun play. She touched the gun in her pocket as she slowly turned.

"What did you say your friend's name was?" the officer asked.

She had to think for a fleeting second that seemed like an eternity. "Umm …" she paused. "Evette … Evette Yates, that's her name." Her voice cracked as she slowly eased her hand out of her pocket.

To her relief, she watched both officers turn and walk briskly back toward their patrol car parked up the street. Gina sighed as she took off in a trot, headed back to the limo. The police turned on their searchlight as they did a U-turn in the middle of the street.

"They're gone," she said, nearly out of breath once she reached the car.

The encounter with the police had somehow left her feeling fatigued and weary. Jack could see she was visibly shaken. Her fake tears had caused her mascara to run and she looked like a sad clown. As she stood outside of the car, she inhaled the strong fumes from the gasoline and made a face at Jack.

"Get in and drive the car to the school near the Marcus Garvey projects. Park in the lot." Jack ordered.

"But …" she was about to complain.

"Just do what da fuck I just said," he hollered.

Prophet continued to moan as he writhed in pain on the floor.

Jack spoke to G-Solo as the car headed to its destination, a killing field. "You're the sole beneficiary of a million dollar empire. With Damon Dice gone, everything falls into your hands, everything that you and him built together, know what I mean," Jack said in an attempt to make G-Solo see the master plan.

"I don't know if Damon is gone yet," G-Solo said somberly.

The car hit a bump in the road. Prophet moaned in agony.

"Big man with the big mouth, it's fitna be over in just a minute," Jack said, looking down at him. He turned back to G-Solo and said to him ominously, with his top lip curled, "Trust me when I say Damon Dice ain't never comin' back. My nigga, believe dat. Now, if you play your cards right, you can inherit the reigns to your seventy-five-million-dollar part of the DieHard throne, or tonight you could lose your life, too," Jack whispered as he leaned over and kicked Prophet in the knee. "You don't wanna be like big mouth here, do ya?" Jack asked.

G-Solo shook his head vigorously like a man who wanted to live.

"The only thing better than the double cross is the triple cross," Jack said, his voice harsh like gravel. "Meaning, three can keep a secret if two are dead. And if Damon and Prophet are gone, the world is yours," Jack said persuasively.

"Don't listen to him," Prophet yelled from the floor.

"Nigga, that's why I'm fitna make your bitch-ass extra crispy," Jack exhorted angrily as he turned back to G-Solo with a feral grin. "Nigga, you tryna die or what?" Jack asked, pointing at G-Solo's head.

"Ye … ye … yes, I wanna live! I want to live! Please don't kill me," G-Solo pleaded with his animated palms shaking in front of him like he was about to go into convulsions.

The car suddenly stopped. Jack peered out of the window and then calmly leaned back in his seat with gun in hand. Casually he lit another cigarette and placed it in his mouth. Gina opened the car door allowing the crescent moon's sinister glow to cover Jack Lemon's ski mask as he held the chrome-plated nine.

"Gimme your gun," Jack said, gesturing to Gina with his hand.

She hesitated and passed it to him. She watched as he took all the bullets out, except one. He got out of the car carefully, checking the infrastructure and its surroundings. They were in the parking lot in back of a school. Jack ordered both men out of the car. Prophet complained that he couldn't walk.

"Okay, have it your way," Jack said nonchalantly as his eyes continued to survey everything around them.

The last thing Jack wanted was a witness to the gruesome horror he was about to inflict on his enemies. He raised the gun to G-Solo's head.

"Dawg, here's the deal. I'm gonna give you the gun with one bullet in it and you're gonna shoot your man in the head with it and give it back to me with your fingerprints all over it. From this day forward you gonna be partnas with some big people in big places. When the police arrive you'll just say you were robbed. Know what I mean?"

G-Solo was shaking so badly that his lips were starting to tremble with the rest of his body. Large beads of perspiration cascaded down his forehead. He managed to nod his head tremulously with a frown on his face, like a man watching doctors perform open hear t surgery on him.

Jack passed him the gun as Gina looked on in utter shock.

"No! No!" Prophet screamed as he somehow managed to crawl out of the car. Jack threw the lit cigarette onto Prophet's gasoline-saturated clothes, igniting them, making Prophet a human fire-ball, an orange blaze lighting up the night. The heat was warm against Gina's arm, causing her to take a step back, aghast at the sight of the burning body.

"Shoot muthafucka, shoot!" Jack yelled at G-Solo.

As G-Solo's hand trembled, he grimaced while tears spilled down his cheeks.

POW!

The gun roared as the bullet caught Prophet just above the right cheek, causing him to roll across the pavement. Suddenly the night had taken on a new meaning. It was wild and primitive as if a beast had been awoken. Prophet continued to thrash about. Jack stepped into the fray and fired five quick, successive shots into Prophet's burning body.

"Die muthafucka, die!" Jack's bestial voice sounded almost inhuman as it resonated throughout the ghetto like a lion's mighty roar or a young gangster staking his claim to the next throne of the streets.

Finally, Prophet's body stopped moving. The fire continued to burn as the awful scent of burnt flesh filled the air.

Gina thought she was going to vomit. The fire flickered off G-Solo's teary eyes as Jack forcefully turned him around. He violently struck G-Solo and shoved the barrel of the gun in his mouth, breaking several of his teeth and possibly his jaw in the process.

Jack spoke with his jaws clenched tightly together as the smog from the smoke bathed both of them. He was intent on getting his point across to G-Solo. He needed to get inside the terrified man's head to make him do as he said.

"Pussy nigga, you said you wanna live. Here's your chance. When the po-pos come, you can tell them you was robbed and your man got killed. You'll spend the rest of your life as a millionaire, not to mention, I'm rewarding your bitch ass with your life. Or you can explain how you murdered both men,

Damon and big mouth," Jack said, nodding toward the smoldering body of Prophet. "Remember, I got the gun to prove it."

G-Solo listened carefully as he choked on the blood spilling from his mouth. He ran his numb tongue over his gums where his

teeth used to be. He was certain that at least seven teeth were missing. "I swear to God, if you let me live, sir, I'll keep my mouth shut. Pleeeeeaze don't kill me," G-Solo gibbered as best he could.

"I'll do whatever you want me to do."

Jack realized that G-Solo was dangerously near delirium. He hoped he hadn't pushed him over the edge. There's only so much terror a mind can take.

Jack spun G-Solo around. "In a week or so when you get out of the hospital from the gunshot wound, a friend is going to pay you a visit at the Tony building."

"Gunshot wound?" G-Solo mouthed.

"Yeah, I gotta make this look real," Jack said.

He nodded toward Gina and she stepped up and removed G-Solo's Rolex.

Blood from his mouth fell on her wrist.

"Dawg, I know mo' than you think I know 'bout 'cha. Yo' mama live in New Jersey with the rest of them fake-ass, wanna-be rappers," Jack added, making yet another threat as he looked around, his eyes alert and his mind telling him he had been here too long. He took a step back and shot G-Solo in the ass.

He screamed and fell to the ground. Jack was just about ready to trot off when he remembered something. He quickly walked over to the trunk of the car and fired two shots into it. He and Gina jogged off into the night, holding hands. Together they had left behind human wreckage, the mayhem of a prominent up-and-coming young gangster whose motto was "Black love first." And, as usual, the streets were watching. Young nigga on the come up.

G-Solo hobbled over to the phone inside the car and dialed 911, reporting that he had been shot and robbed and that his bodyguard had been murdered. As he spoke into the phone, a cinder from the fire was still burning. G-Solo reached over and pushed the button to open the trunk. The chauffeur had somehow managed to survive. He had been shot in the legs.

Moments later, the authorities arrived. Lieutenant Anthony Brown was with them. Three men had been shot, one of them fatally. One of the victims had actually been burnt to a crisp. Leonard Green, better known as G-Solo, had clearly developed a bad case of amnesia. All he could remember was a masked gunman and a woman. Judging from the evidence at the crime scene, Lieutenant Brown recognized an execution-style hit. He had been living in Brooklyn long enough to see that right away. Now he just wondered why G-Solo hadn't been killed. Someone wanted to keep him alive, but why?

Made in the USA
Lexington, KY
11 October 2014